Perfect P

© Copyright © 2020 Mered

Chapter One

It was a cold night in December when James Daniels came home drunk. He clumsily got out of his Uber and walked up the chunky stairs to his swanky flat in Chelsea. The bright white bricks and large windows marked the property as somewhere exclusive.

Inside his home, he threw himself on the leather sofa, still feeling the good vibes from the night which had just commenced. He was sure he had got a phone number of a pretty girl with long hair, but that was nothing new to James. His money and good looks spoke for him when it came to the opposite sex.

As James thought about the night, he looked at his phone to see the pretty girl had texted him. He didn't reply. Instead, he used the inner light that burned inside of him to ignite the ability to shapeshift. As his body buzzed and tingled, he instantly morphed into a huge grey wolf.

The wolf that James turned into was a fierce and powerful-looking creature. As the brilliant beast, James leapt onto the leather sofa. The feel of its smooth texture against his fur was wonderful. In his animal form, he was excited as he rolled upon the sofa.

Feeling the intoxication from the alcohol and the amazing buzz he would always get when he changed, his tail wagged and his grey paws moved around like he was a giddy puppy.

He jumped off the sofa and ran into the kitchen, where he searched on the counters as though he was really a wolf foraging for food in a deserted house. He loved how morphing into a wolf gave him the sense of a blurred thought process. His mind would normally work in words and feelings. Yet when he was in the guise of an animal, it was in colours and hot flashes of emotion.

His urge was to have food. With his strong nose, he pushed open the fridge and sniffed around. The fridge was full of groceries, which the canine gorged on, pulling out whatever he could from the fridge. He was enjoying being this wild animal.

After he had demolished all that he could eat, he drank from a water bowl that James himself had left in the kitchen because he often enjoyed shapeshifting and knew he would need this.

The wolf form of James wagged its tail in a slow manner as he made his way to the large bedroom. Upon the satin sheets, James lay down as a wolf, rolling around until the drowsy feelings from the alcohol and the shapeshifting took over. It had been a long day of work and play.

The wolf curled up on the satin sheets where he slept, dreaming strange dreams of what it would be like to chase little rabbits and truly embody the wolf's spirit.

When he awoke in the morning, James was back in his human form. His body was naked. He was a lean man of medium frame. His shoulder-length brown hair was untidy as he lay on the bed.

Hearing the annoying buzz of his alarm on his phone from the living room, he jumped off the bed.

'Oh crap,' he said, as he turned the alarm off. It was seven in the morning.

James undressed in his bathroom, where he stepped into a hot shower. His muscular body enjoyed the hot water as it caressed over his skin. He washed his hair and body. In the shower, he thought about how much he had enjoyed turning into a wolf; it had been the best part of a great night. It was then that he realised it was a Saturday and he didn't have to get up so early.

'God, I'm such a muppet,' he said, laughing to himself as he stepped out of the shower.

He quickly dried his hair and brushed his teeth. Looking in the mirror at his fine features, he smiled. He really was an extremely good-looking man, who wouldn't look out of place in a fashion magazine.

'I suppose I could get on with my day,' he said to himself, as he dressed in jogging bottoms and a black Calvin Klein shirt.

James poured himself a black coffee, which he slowly sipped as he checked his emails on his sleek MacBook computer.

'Glad it's not a work day,' James said, as he looked through the business reports that he would deal with on Monday.

James had come from money. His father Earl had inherited it from his own father. James had never known an uncomfortable day in his life when in regards to material things.

Yet James had also landed a good job on his academic merit. He had studied Business at the London School of Economics, where he gained a first-class degree. He was a bright man who enjoyed the business world.

He was good at his job, where he worked in a PR department for an advertising company in central London. He had been working there for two years and loved the job. He earned around forty thousand a year, which wouldn't be enough to live in a £2-million flat, yet his father had bought it for him when he turned eighteen.

James had the perfect life. He was healthy, rich and popular. He also had a double life, because he was a morph. A magical shapeshifting creature. He had also inherited this from his father Earl.

After checking his work emails, he logged in to his personal emails. A lot of them were junk from his gym and other places, but he enjoyed checking them. Agnes had emailed him about meeting up soon, which he was pleased about, as he always enjoyed seeing her.

He emailed his friend Bradley about meeting that night. It was early in the morning, so he didn't expect a reply just yet.

I could go to the gym, or I could go back to bed, James said to himself, as he walked towards his bed. It was covered in wolf hairs. *Just my luck*, he thought, then made his way to the other bedroom. He generally used it for guests, but on this occasion, it would have to do.

James got comfortable in the small single bed and yawned in a lazy, carefree sort of way. He found it easy to fall back to sleep, where he dreamed of being the wolf once more.

James awoke to his phone ringing at noon. It was his best friend Bradley, who he had known since middle school.

'What's up, Bradley?' he asked.

'Good night?' his friend enquired on the other end of the phone.

'It was all right. I had a few drinks, few laughs, you know.'

'Yeah. Sounds about right. Do you want to go out tonight? It would be good to catch up on things,' Bradley said.

'Sounds like a plan,' James said, and as they continued to converse, they arranged what time they would meet.

James had always liked Bradley. He had a soft nature and gentle wit about him. He was bright and funny. James had never revealed to Bradley what he was. No one would believe it unless they saw it, and anyone who saw it wouldn't be believed by anyone they told!

*****

James met Bradley at the swanky Mayfair Club an hour before it became packed. Bradley was tall, with soft features and naturally ginger hair. He was a good-looking guy but wasn't as much of an extrovert as his best friend James.

'Good to see you're back from your trip in one piece!' James exclaimed, as he hugged his friend.

'It was amazing travelling around Spain. Brushing up on my Spanish and seeing all the incredible sights. I took some great photos as well,' Bradley said, smiling brightly.

'Meet any pretty senoritas?'

Bradley made a face. 'No, I didn't. I talked to some nice-looking girls, but no one I felt, you know … that spark with.'

'Spanish girls are known for their beauty. Did you hook up with anyone?'

'No. You know it's not my style, one night stands and that kind of crap,' Bradley said.

'Fair enough. Well, maybe you'll meet someone nice tonight, eh.'

'I doubt it. Let's just enjoy the night and catch up,' Bradley said.

Bradley told James all about travelling around Spain. How he had taken a three-month course to improve his Spanish. Bradley had studied the language as part of his A levels before he went to university.

Both of the men were thirty years of age. They were both from privileged backgrounds. Their family homes had been in Mayfair, and that's how they had met in middle school. They had then spent many years in the same private schools up until sixth form.

When they both went to different universities in their late teens, they had kept in touch. They had never really had a time in their lives when they didn't meet up with each other or keep in touch regularly through phone calls.

James regarded Bradley as his best friend. Bradley knew everything about James's nature, such as how he was with women and what he valued in life. The only secret Bradley was completely oblivious to was that James belonged to a supernatural world.

They enjoyed the quiet and sophisticated air of the club. This was the sort of venue where a Malibu and coke was ten pounds and the bouncers would never dream of letting it get horribly packed.

As people began to mosey on into the club, the two friends remained sitting in the far corner, where they could observe the people who entered. Bradley had a pint of beer and James drank a vodka-based concoction. The two friends felt at ease and in their comfort zone.

As the night progressed, two girls entered. They immediately caught Bradley's eye. They were both fairly tall and slender. One of them had long, golden blonde hair and the other curly brown hair. They were both very pretty girls, yet it was the blonde girl who Bradley regarded as truly stunning.

She was wearing a red jumper dress and her long hair touched her waist. She was talking with the brunette and had relaxed body language.

'Look at those two girls; I think the blonde one is really extra beautiful,' whispered Bradley.

'Go up and say hi,' his friend suggested with a smile.

'Oh, I'm too shy,' remarked Bradley.

'Fine, I'll go and get us some more drinks,' James said, and jumped out of his seat.

Instead of going to the bar, he walked over to the two girls when Bradley's attention was on his smartphone. James thought how they were both pretty girls, yet the blonde was dressed much sexier.

'Hi,' James said.

'Hi there,' said the blonde girl. The other girl simply half-smiled.

'Could my friend and I buy you two a drink?'

'Sure,' said the blonde.

'That's my friend over there,' James said, pointing to Bradley, who was still looking at his phone and hadn't noticed James talking with the girls.

The two girls made their way with James to where Bradley was sitting. He looked up and smiled shyly.

'Er, hi,' said Bradley.

'I thought it would be nice to get talking, my name is James and this is my friend Bradley.'

'I'm Jessica and this is my sister Eliza,' said the blonde.

Bradley smiled nervously at Jessica. He thought how she was even more beautiful up close, with emerald green eyes.

'I'll go and get us all some drinks, what would you ladies like?' asked James.

'A glass of red wine would be nice,' Jessica said.

'And you?' James asked, addressing Eliza.

'The same would be fine, thanks,' said Eliza.

As James left the table, Bradley was left sitting alone with the two beautiful girls. Bradley's mind raced through how he could woo the blonde without seeming rude to her brunette sister.

'So, where are you ladies from?' he asked with a smile, gazing at Jessica for just a moment longer then he meant to.

'We're from Chesham in Buckinghamshire,' Jessica said.

'Oh, nice. And what do you do?' Bradley asked.

'I'm an assistant manager at the local Superdrug. I love retail but it's not what I expected to do after my studies. It just seems to be where I've wound up, you know?' Jessica said with a smile.

'Yeah, I … I know what you mean. What did you study before working in Superdrug? Oh, and that's good that you're enjoying your work,' Bradley said, feeling butterflies dance in his stomach as his eyes focused on her lips, which were coloured in pink lipstick.

'I studied a Bachelor of Arts in Fashion Design,' Jessica said with a smile. 'I love making dresses and things like that. I've always known that's what I want to do with my life.'

'Amazing. That's such a creative thing to study. And yourself, Eliza, what do you do for work or study?' he asked, knowing he needed to include her sister in the conversation.

'I'm still studying. I'm in the final year of a Master's degree in Fine Arts,' Eliza said, speaking more quietly than her sister.

'Oh, excellent. Two creative young women!' Bradley exclaimed, feeling his remark came out sounding cheesy.

James then arrived back with the drinks. He had a tray with all four beverages balanced on it.

Bradley filled in James regarding what they had been talking about, introducing him to what Eliza and Jessica had studied. He was secretly scared that James might woo Jessica for himself.

James introduced himself to the two girls, telling them how he had studied Business and was working in marketing. When it was Bradley's turn to describe himself, his mouth went dry and it took him a minute to compose himself before explaining he was an Economics graduate who loved photography and travel.

'Oh, that's nice,' said Jessica, 'what sort of things do you like taking pictures of?' she asked, smiling at Bradley.

Bradley blushed a deep pink, which was accentuated by his fair complexion. 'Well, anything that catches my eye. I love taking photos of people I meet on my travels, if they let me. Anyone really, I like to think I see the beauty in everyone.'

'That's lovely, Bradley,' Jessica said.

The night seemed to move fast as the conversation picked up. Bradley made every effort to include Eliza, who seemed quiet and uninterested in either of the two men. It was Jessica who Bradley found simply captivating, with her naturally tanned skin and golden blonde hair.

Jessica had a cute laugh, which Bradley found infectious, and he told a funny story about the time when a Yorkshire Terrier had chased him out of a shop in Spain. It was a squeaky laugh that was as cute as a button.

As they enjoyed each other's company, time seemed to sweetly pass by. Jessica gazed back at Bradley, which excited him.

'We should be leaving soon. We've got to catch the Metropolitan line train to Chesham,' Jessica said.

'Um, I …' Bradley babbled, 'I could leave you my number, if you'd like?'

'I'd really like that,' she said, and they exchanged numbers.

As the two girls left the bar, Bradley found his hands were shaking. He had really liked Jessica.

'She seemed to really like you,' James said.

The bar wasn't closing for another hour. The two men ordered themselves a few more beers and chatted about this and that. Just as they ordered an Uber back to James's flat, Bradley made a little noise and jumped in the air.

'What's the matter, man?' asked James with a laugh.

'It's Jessica. She's not only texted me, but suggested we meet next week.'

'I told you she liked you,' James said.

The two men got an Uber back to Chelsea. In James's property, they had food and continued to chat. Bradley exclaimed how he was nervous about the prospect of a date with the beautiful young woman.

'Just be yourself, you're a great guy, Brad,' said James.

Chapter Two

Jessica and her sister waited for the late train back to Chesham. The night had been interesting. Jessica had met a guy that she had instantly clicked with.

As the two slim girls stood waiting for the Metropolitan train at Baker Street station, they chatted amongst themselves about the night.

'He seemed to really like you,' said Eliza with a smile.

'He did, didn't he? He was really cute,' Jessica replied, beaming.

'He also had a very endearing personality. Just take your time to get to know him,' Eliza said.

'Yes, yes, of course. Heartache is so easy to come by in this day and age,' Jessica said, as she tossed her long blonde hair into a high ponytail. She was wearing a red size ten coat that emphasized her beautiful looks.

As the two girls boarded the train, they sat opposite each other. It was a Friday night and the train was full of merry commuters on their way back to Buckinghamshire. Eliza smiled at her sister as she put her headphones in to listen to some music and drown out the sound of drunk men and women laughing and talking.

When the two young women got back to Chesham, it was midnight. They ordered a cab back to the house where they lived with their mother and father. It was a tidy, three-bedroom council property, which the girls had lived in all their lives.

Arriving back home, they found their mother was still up watching TV. Moreen Barnet was a friendly woman who was proud of her daughters.

She had photos of them decorating the living room and hallway. She loved her two girls fiercely.

'In here,' called Moreen.

'Hi, Mum,' Jessica said, as she gave her mum a little hug.

'How was your night, girls?' Moreen asked. The family's tabby cat Chloe was sitting on her lap.

'Really good, Mum. We got talking to these two guys; they were pretty posh, to be honest, but very easy to talk to. Anyway, I really clicked with one of them. His name was Bradley.'

'Oooh,' Moreen said, huffing, 'what did he look like?'

'He was really attractive. Had naturally ginger hair and really lovely facial features,' Jessica said.

'And a great personality,' Eliza added; she was sitting on the flowery sofa, checking through her phone.

'Sounds good. Did you meet anyone nice?' Moreen addressed Eliza.

Eliza pulled a face. 'No, Mum. I don't think my type of guy frequents such a snazzy bar.'

'Oh, Eliza. You're a lovely-looking girl. You need to be more like your sister Jessica. Smile a bit more and stop hiding your figure,' her mother exclaimed.

'Mum!' Eliza said, laughing in mock outrage. 'With that, I'll be off to bed. I've got an essay on

Frida Kahlo to finish tomorrow. So, I'll go and get some sleep.'

'Goodnight, dear,' Moreen said.

Eliza went upstairs as her mother and sister continued to talk about the cute guy that Jessica had met.

Eliza was glad to be back in her room. As she looked in the mirror, she removed what little make-up she had on. She had perfect skin, so really didn't need to use foundation. She wore a tiny bit of mascara and a little lip balm.

As she undressed and got into her pyjamas, she thought to herself about the night. She didn't want to be like her sister Jessica. Her mother often favoured Jessica because she looked exactly like Moreen had done in her youth. Her mother never said it, yet it was something that Eliza felt in her heart. Her mother had never had a problem finding a husband and wasn't the shy type. Jessica was like Moreen in that respect; she was a very confident woman.

Eliza's room was extremely tidy. She was a graduate student in Fine Arts and her room held a large easel, where she did her paintings on canvas. Eliza's style of art was bold and often abstract. She loved painting with great passion.

As she turned off the light and got into her single bed, her mind easily switched off and entered dreamland. There she dreamed of a black shadow walking behind her. In the dream, the shadow was that of a man. It was the oddest dream.

*****

James Daniel was to meet with his guide Agnes that afternoon. All of his kind were given one. All shapeshifting morphs needed a guide to teach them how to harness their powers.

A guide was summoned from some place magical when a morph was born. It was known that they forgot their charges once that morph died. The memories went into a pendant that they wore. From the old books on mythology which James had read, he knew that a guide would only remember all their charges once they retired from their mystical duties for good.

Agnes was in her sixties and had always been a fat woman, with short hair that had flecks of blonde in its colour. She had always smiled and cooed over James when he had been a little boy. He thought fondly about how he'd always loved her.

She was a mother figure to him. His own mother had died when he had been only a few weeks old. He knew little about her. His father didn't like to talk about his late wife.

Agnes rang the doorbell. James eagerly answered. When he saw her little round face and bright blue eyes, he felt a sense of peace and happiness.

'It's so good to see you,' he said, as he hugged Agnes.

'Yes, yes. It's always fantastic seeing you. Now, let me get in before the cold air outside gives me some sort of a fever,' Agnes said, making her way into the flat, where she threw herself down on the black leather sofa.

'How was your guide summit in Nashville?'

'Oh, you know. There's gossip galore at those things. Drinks, too. People showing off about how well their morph charges are doing. "Oooh, and she's met a fairy queen in the magical realm" or "Oooh, he's got a job here on Earth as an accountant", you know the sort of gossip that occurs at those events,' Agnes said with a grin.

'I can only imagine,' said James with a chuckle.

The magical realm was a dimension where all magical beings descended from. It was believed there were numerous parallel dimensions, yet Earth and the magical realm had been connected together for untold eons of time. All the myths about witches, werewolves and vampires came from people who had encountered beings who came to this world from the magical realm.

James was one such being. He and his father were morphs. Shapeshifting beings who could wield the elements to create magical occurrences. Unlike a witch, they did not need spells to cast magical events.

'Now tell me, why did I feel a change in the air for you?' Agnes asked, surveying her charge with a friendly yet enquiring glance.

'I really cannot think why you'd feel a change in the air. There's nothing new to report. I have been enjoying work, partying a bit, you know – the usual.'

'Well, I felt some sort of change in the air. I would advise you to do some soul-searching and look over events that have taken place in your life recently. Something important has happened in your destiny.'

James snorted. 'I'll retrace my steps.'

Agnes and James talked about the guide summit in Nashville. Agnes had loads of gossip to bestow upon James, which he enjoyed listening to. They drank champagne and laughed a lot.

Later that evening, they went out to a fine Italian restaurant that they were both fond of in Mayfair. James had booked them a quiet table downstairs in the restaurant. Politicians and celebrities were the type of people who could afford to regularly eat at such an exclusive restaurant.

They ordered finely cooked pasta and more champagne. A skilled violinist was playing downstairs in the restaurant. The music the man played was fine and melodic.

'I love it here. I love seeing you, my little dumpling, and what a handsome man you are growing up to be,' Agnes cooed.

'Stop,' he said, laughing. 'I love seeing you, too.'

'Stop, you say,' she replied with a wink, and with a wave of her hand, she stopped time in its track. The music stopped and the movement of everything in the restaurant froze except for James and herself. They watched as even the candle on the table was frozen in motion.

'The whole world's frozen for just a moment,' said Agnes with a giggle.

'Yes, I know. It's one of the greatest party tricks of a magical being's repertoire,' James said.

Agnes waved her hand and time swiftly fell back into place. The music continued to play as if nothing had happened, and people commenced eating and talking around them.

'Now, you do it,' Agnes said.

'If I must,' James said with a sigh.

'Yes, you must. I must see you show me your energies are in good order.'

James made a face and then he blinked and time stood still. Agnes wriggled in her seat and exclaimed how proud she was of him. She loved seeing him illustrate his morph powers.

'Well done, my boy,' she said.

'Yes, well. I'm doing good, or else I wouldn't be able to concentrate enough to do that, would I?' James enquired with a smirk.

'Is everything all right?' Agnes asked.

'It's just … I've been thinking about, you know, what I am. I'm not just a morph, am I …'

'Yes, of course. You are your mother's son, after all,' Agnes said with a sigh.

'I just worry it will get in the way of me finding someone to love,' James confessed. It was something he hadn't shared with Agnes before.

'Oh. What nonsense. You've all of the magical realm to find a woman … or even here on Earth, perhaps. You have the choice of two worlds and looks that could kill. You're never much single anyway, but for the matter of finding a woman with the material for a wife … well, you need to assess what it is you are truly looking for.'

'Could they love a man that's half-vampire though?' James asked, feeling rotten thinking about secrets he held from Agnes. About his identity and how it shaped how he saw the world. In ways a normal morph man wouldn't see life. He felt there was too much evil at his core.

'Women can love all sort of monsters. Your father married your mother and she was a full vampire. I know we don't talk about these things much. Yet rest assured, my precious one … true love is something I believe will come your way one of these days.'

James blinked hard, feeling his concentration waver. Time came back into being and the two changed the subject from his vampire heritage to just simply talking about finding love. A subject which anyone could discuss in a restaurant.

'Love is something that is hard to find for everyone. Even someone as shockingly handsome as yourself,' Agnes said.

'I really hope you are right,' James said.

They talked on many things that night as they continue to enjoy each other's company. Agnes stopped time once more to replicate her meal, so they wouldn't have to pay for a second portion! It wasn't that they couldn't afford it; it was simply that she liked to show off with her magic. She also had the appetite to match her large body. She was a hefty woman.

James used his magic to take away any influence of the alcohol and drove them home in his silver sports car. Feeling the joy of being perfectly sober and listening to Agnes giggle to herself was a nice feeling. The drive was swift and soon they were back at his Chelsea flat.

He'd already made up the spare room just the way Agnes liked it. He had put potpourii by the drawer and now lit a scented candle that would burn just until she fell asleep – the joy of magic!

'You've had a long day,' James said, as he hugged Agnes. 'Tomorrow we will go shopping and I will get you whatever you want.'

'Oh goodness. My boy spoils me. Goodnight,' she said, as she made her way to the spare room.

When James was alone, he looked at his phone. He had messages from acquaintances and business partners who he regarded well. Yet one message that made him smile was from his best friend Bradley. His friend told him how he had gone on a date with that girl Jessica that they both had met on Friday.

James smiled to himself thinking of Bradley. He sometimes wished he could tell him about his morph heritage, yet mortals weren't allowed to know about the secrets of those who came to this world from the magical realm. He knew that Bradley would only be upset by the knowledge.

James was lucky. Not only did he have a wonderful life on Earth with good friends and a great job; he had a whole other life that he could enjoy any time he wanted.

With the key, which was invisible to all who knew not of the magical realm, James could enter this dimension any time he was alone. He could enter it in a toilet cubicle and for not even a second would it appear that he had gone, yet hundreds of years might have passed. When he came back to

Earth, time would have stood still for the entire duration, as that was part of the incredible magic that stood between these two dimensions.

There were times that he would be in a boring meeting and, once it was over, he would quickly slip to the bathroom, where he would take a break in the magical realm and go exploring. He would spend a whole day just enjoying his life there and then return to work feeling refreshed and enjoy the rest of his day on Earth!

Tonight, James took his key and opened the door. Agnes was sleeping in the other room, yet she too could enter the magical realm as she pleased. She also had one of the invisible keys.

He found himself in his house, where his key opened into the realm. Nothing had changed since he had last been at home two weeks previously. Not a stitch in time; everything was waiting for him to continue.

He didn't feel like much. He just wanted to sleep in his bed in his home in Locgarden, a bustling city in this realm. His house was a large palace, as he was affluent in both realities. It was painted in deep purples and had an open plan design, as the city was hot most of the year.

He chose his favourite bedroom to sleep in. In his room away from a world where his identity was a secret, he found he slept well. He dreamt of a beautiful woman, whose face he could not decipher, walking briskly away from him. In the dream, he desperately felt the urge to follow her.

Yet when the sun rose in Locgarden, he forgot the dream. He felt refreshed and joyful as he prepared breakfast. He checked his phone, the one that belonged to this realm, seeing messages from Neava. It made him feel excitement to think of the next time he would see his mistress.

The blue-haired beauty would have to wait until another time. He closed the door behind him on the magical realm and stepped back into his flat in Chelsea.

Not even a second had gone by there, yet he was rested and had slept for a long time in Locgarden. He decided to get to work on emails that needed to be answered and reports that needed looking over for work.

As Agnes slept, he felt more at ease. Yes, he was a morph and also a vampire, but he had almost everything he wanted. Surely that was enough to make any man happy.

Chapter Three

James was happy to greet Agnes when she woke at ten in the morning. He brought her coffee and cooked her a breakfast when she waddled into the living room.

'Oh, dear boy, I sense you've been to the magical realm,' she said, still sleepy but beaming.

'I spent a night resting there. Just in my room at my house over there. It was nice just to clear my head of things. My life over there is waiting for me just as much as this one,' he said, as he handed her the black coffee with two sugars.

'Perfect coffee,' she said, sipping from the white mug. 'Yes, I understand completely. But I feel that whatever stirring I had, where my senses told me something in your destiny had come into place, wasn't in the magical realm.'

'Well, I really can't think of anything that has happened of late that would be of importance in my destiny. I'll do some soul-searching and retrace my steps like I promised.'

It was an enjoyable Sunday in London town. James took Agnes to Bond Street, where he bought her Chanel perfume and a locket from the designer boutique. She wasn't much of a shopper and had had enough after visiting this one exclusive shop.

They had lunch in a smart café. They stopped time just once during their visit to the café, to discuss how James was to retrace his steps and look at what might be needed to unearth important elements of his destiny.

After that, they went to the West End, where they watched *Wicked*. Neither of them had seen the musical before and they enjoyed it very much. James felt at peace when he was with Agnes. She was a truly wonderful guide and he was very lucky to have someone so accepting in his life.

She was all too aware that he was not a pure morph. His father was a morph through and through, yet his mother had been a vampire. Agnes was his guide because of his morph heritage. They didn't often talk about what being a vampire meant to James.

Agnes knew full well that he had the bloodlust. She knew he had taken classes at Locgarden's School of the Supernatural in the magical realm, where he would have been taught to supress dark urges.

Yet her concern was bringing him up to be a morph. He wasn't the typical morph, yet he was still her charge. She loved him dearly and took her work very seriously.

After the show in London, they went back to James's flat. Tomorrow night, she would be leaving James and having free time until he should call on her. She eagerly awaited those calls. He had finished his lessons with her and only required morph training in magic every so often to hone his powers.

When Monday morning came around, James woke to find that Agnes had already left. She had left him a note stating that she was going to travel around Japan until he should call upon her. Due to Agnes's magical powers, she would enter Japan fully fluent in the language.

James smiled to himself as he made a cup of tea. He had work later on that day, yet a smile crept across his face as he thought about taking a little detour to the magical realm before he had to go to the office.

As his flat was now completely empty, he took out his key that was on a chain only visible to other magical beings. He opened a doorway to his house in Locgarden and stepped into the magical realm.

As the gateway behind him closed, he smiled as he smelled the beautiful incense present in his home. No time had passed since he had last been sleeping there a day ago.

'I think I'll give Neava a call,' he said to himself, feeling excited at the prospect of seeing her again.

Neava was his. She had signed a contract to only belong to him in exchange for enough money to never require to work again. She had a house nearby his own home, on a street that was particularly well known for belonging to mortals who knew of the supernatural truths of the magical realm.

Some mortals would deny the truths that were semi-hidden from the humans of this world. They would say that the 'vampires' and 'witches' were simply myths. They denied that there was magic flowing through every inch of this realm.

Yet there were also a lot of mortals such as Neava, who had always accepted the truth of the realm. The realm was called 'the magical realm' by those supernatural beings. Yet most mortals called it simply 'the realm' and had their own theological beliefs to explain how the world worked.

Neava was a beautiful woman in her mid-twenties. She was five years younger than James. With naturally electric dark blue hair that glittered bright in the sunlight and amazing deep brown eyes, she was certainly a beauty.

She had met James when she was sixteen. She hadn't known he was a supernatural being but had been instantly interested in him. He had compelled her to give herself to him completely, yet when the compulsion wore off, she was happy enough to do this of her own free will.

James was so pleased that she answered the phone at once. He felt a buzzing energy in his stomach as he thought about her and heard her voice.

'Master?' Neava enquired, in her soft, seductive voice.

'Want to visit me?' James asked.

'Well, of course. Shall I come to the house now?' she asked.

'Come right away,' James said.

'Yes, master. I'll be there soon.'

James put down his phone and changed into more fitting clothes. He wore brown trousers made of a soft material. He wore a purple shirt that was loose and matching the styles fashionable in Locgarden and the realm beyond the great city.

When Neava arrived, she was wearing a white dress that sat just below her knees. Her arms were exposed, and her tanned olive skin looked healthy and glowing.

James motioned for her to come in. As he closed the door, she flung her arms around him. They kissed passionately and soon words didn't seem important. They found themselves in the bedroom, where they made passionate love.

James didn't love Neava, but he liked her as much as one could like a beautiful girl with all the exciting assets of wit and intelligence that she possessed in great quantities.

After being together, James showered alone and Neava bathed in the other room. He needed time on his own to reflect on the strange thoughts that were swirling through his mind.

It was something to do with the dream he had had the other night in this home. Something about a girl with brown hair. Could it be that he was thinking about those two girls he had met the other night?

'What's on your mind?' Neava asked.

James was finishing dressing and getting ready to soon go back to work in London.

'It's nothing. I'm going to get back to the other realm, I've work to do. I'll be back soon. Stay here; you know it will feel only a second until I'm back.'

'Of course,' Neava said with a smile.

James left the room and opened the doorway back to his life on Earth. He left for work and sailed through the day of meetings and pitches for new advertising projects. He enjoyed his work, yet his mind was on Eliza.

Should he contact her? Should he reach out to her in some way? What did he even see in her? Yes, she was a beauty, but her sister had been the more noticeable of the two women.

Was it her sophistication? How she was studying and passionate about what she was pursuing?

Whatever the case, when he got home from work, he searched on Facebook for Bradley.

Bradley had only just entered a relationship with Eliza's sister Jessica. They had only been on one date. He hoped his friend wouldn't mind him reaching out to Eliza.

Feeling anticipation, he quickly sent a friend request to Eliza. Her profile picture illustrated her fine features and the fact that she was unaware just how pretty she was.

James stepped back into the magical realm, where he spent some more time with Neava, who had only been waiting a moment for him.

'Was your day at work good?' she asked.

'Yes, the best. It was brilliant, thanks for asking.'

He requested that he taste Neava just a little. She wasn't keen on letting him drink her blood, but always knew he would never harm her. Handing over her arm to him, he gently took it in his hand.

As he moved his mouth over her olive skin and drew his fangs to the surface, she gasped as he delved through her skin to access her blood.

He only took the slightest amount, drinking from her for only a second. Yet for both of them the gentle drinking of a vampire was something of pure ecstasy.

Chapter Four

Neava walked home to her modest yet comfortable home in Locgarden. She was still buzzing from the sensation of James taking some of her blood. It left her whole body singing with pleasure.

She knew he had always regarded her as a possession of fun. Yet his magic had protected her life and meant that no harm could ever come to her until her time of death was naturally upon her.

At home, she made herself a brew of herbal tea that James had told her about. She had bought it from a witches' market. The tea was supposed to create bliss in the person who drank it.

As the herbs danced in the hot water, Neava let the drink cool. She thought about how she enjoyed the experiences of bliss she found with James. He was her master and she had always given herself to him.

She had never experienced romance of any kind with any other man. James was one hell of a man because of his powers. Being a vampire, he was dangerous, and his regard for her as a thing to be protected and enjoyed was something that made her feel sexy.

Yet friends around her had distanced themselves from the blue-haired beauty, calling her 'a women of the night' or a 'slut'. She had indeed sold her virginity and sexual self to James for all her life. The contract was bound in magic and she wouldn't have even been able to break it if she had wished to.

As she sipped the tea, the feelings of self-doubt and worldly worries slipped away. She laughed as the spices tickled her throat and made her whole body zing with happiness.

She left her house and walked through Locgarden, enjoying the night on a crazy-good high. She was the one that James wanted. She knew that he had other women in the world beyond this world, yet none of those relationships were serious. No one had known him for as long as she had. No one could love him like she did.

*****

James was pleased to find that Eliza had accepted his friend request on Facebook. He looked through her pictures. There were photos of her with Jessica and her mother, who looked like a fat and older version of Jessica.

He smiled to himself as he saw photos of her undergraduate graduation ceremony. He gazed upon her gentle beauty and noted how none of the pictures were trying to be sexy.

James was thirty years old and Eliza was in her late twenties. She was obviously a sophisticated woman. He saw no indication in her photos that she was in a relationship.

'Hi,' he typed in the private messages, awaiting the next step where he could initiate some sort of contact with her.

He felt anticipation dance in his body as he awaited her reply. It took an hour for her to respond, in which time he had consumed a can of Pepsi and watched the news on TV.

'Hi, James,' she typed back.

James nervously responded, feeling his hands shake. What was it about this woman that made him so curious? She certainly wasn't his normal type; she was too modest.

James expressed how he thought it would be nice for the two of them to meet. He stated how he was interested in art and curious to talk with someone who knew so much about the subject.

Eliza accepted his invitation to meet. They arranged to meet at Harrow-on-the-hill train station on Wednesday evening.

*****

Eliza had lectures on Wednesday. She sat in the main lecture hall, where the art students were all gathered to listen to a talk on Art History. As she sat with her laptop in front of her to type up notes on, she was dressed in a pencil skirt and a grey shirt, and wore a red cardigan. She looked elegant and more dressed up than her usual attire for university.

After class she was to meet with James Daniels. She had been very shocked to receive a friend request from him. She had thought he hadn't regarded her at all when they had met.

She felt nervous at the prospect of being in his company once again. Those chocolate brown eyes of his were almost hypnotising. She remembered how she had felt uncomfortable to even make the slightest conversation when they had met at the bar in Mayfair.

After the lecture, she turned off her laptop and put it in her bag. She walked to the train station in silence and took the trains that led her back to Harrow on the Hill. This was the route she always took to get back to Chesham.

Yet today, she was meeting James before going home. She was not planning on telling her mother, who would imply that it was some sort of date. Eliza was sure that it was no such thing, yet she had worn her best underwear and finest Dior perfume.

She had never been intimate with a man. Something only her close family and few friends knew about her. She was twenty-eight years old and intimacy frightened her. She was scared of the possibility of rejection and the idea of being so close to someone.

When she arrived at Harrow on the Hill station, James was waiting outside. He was standing next to a silver sports car.

He was dressed in a black coat and jeans. She could see just a flicker of his white linen shirt. He looked like a male model. Eliza felt embarrassed to be seen with him. She felt as though she would be in his shadow.

'Good to see you again,' James said.

'Yes, same to you,' Eliza said.

James walked forward to her; Eliza felt her heart beat faster. 'Shall we get some food and talk there?' he asked.

'Sounds fine,' she replied.

'You'll have to pick a restaurant, as I've not really been to Harrow often. I had a few friends from university attend school here.'

Of course – Harrow School! Eliza thought, thinking of how both James and Bradley were wealthy men who had experienced private education.

Eliza showed James to the local Pizza Express, which was in one of the shopping centres in Harrow. He walked casually and confidently behind her, with no indication that he was embarrassed to be in her company.

The restaurant wasn't especially packed. They sat opposite each other. James smiled at her and his eyes were bright with warmth; yet Eliza felt too nervous to smile back.

'You look well, Eliza,' James said.

'Thank you,' she said.

The waiter came by and they both ordered the same vegetarian pizza. James decided to have a glass of red wine and Eliza asked for sparkling water.

'Not much for wine?' James asked.

'I'm going to be working on my dissertation later tonight. I haven't got class tomorrow, so I want to make use of the night,' she said, which was very true. Eliza liked to work on her research.

'You're studying for a Master's, is that right?' James asked.

'Yes, that's correct,' she said, shocked that he remembered, as she didn't have her educational information on her Facebook.

'Smart girl. Remind me where you're studying?'

'Chelsea School of Art,' Eliza said with a blush.

James smiled at her once more. 'That's near where I live. Tell me, is that where you studied your undergraduate degree as well?'

'No. That was at the University of East London. I studied Fine Arts for my Bachelor of Arts also. It's always been my absolute favourite subject.'

'That's wonderful,' said James, beaming. 'So, what sort of art do you produce?'

Eliza felt shy talking about her art, yet also excited to reveal who she was to this incredibly handsome man. 'I paint abstract art. Most of my works are portraits of faces of human or humanoid beings. I love working with paint.'

'I'd love to see your work.'

'I guess … I could send you a photograph of one of my latest pieces,' Eliza commented, blushing.

'I would sincerely love that,' James said.

When the waiter came over with their food, Eliza wasn't really hungry, as she felt nervous being herself around James. He asked her who her favourite painters were. She told him how she loved Frida Kahlo.

James talked about his work. He told Eliza how he enjoyed working in marketing. They mostly talked about art and what painters they both liked.

Eliza expressed how she collected prints from random artists around the world. She told him how she also loved photography and was always taking photos.

'Do you have an Instagram account?' James asked. 'I'd love to see your photographs.'

Eliza shyly shared her Instagram handle, which she used to show her art and photography. She was shy to let him see her art, which meant the world to her. Her art was an extension of herself. It was such a great part of her personality.

James got out his iPhone and followed her handle on Instagram. He made a little more small talk but soon their meal was finished and it was time that Eliza got the train home.

She felt a sense of sadness as they said goodbye. As he got into his car and she made her way up the stairs to wait for the train, she wondered if she would ever see him again.

Eliza's sister Jessica was happily dating his friend Bradley. They were in the earliest stages of dating, yet it seemed unlikely that James would wish to spend another evening with her. She imagined he found her dull and too homely for her to ignite any interest from him.

*****

James was happy with how the evening had gone. He had made more contact with Eliza, who was such an interesting and refined woman. They were from very different class backgrounds. He lived in a flat that cost £2 million, which his father had bought for him, and she lived in a council property. He did not know whether her parents owned their own home or not, nor did he care. What interested him was just how lovely Eliza was in looks and personality.

He knew that he really liked her. He was frightened of appearing too keen. When he got home, he sent her a Facebook message saying it had been nice to see her.

He wanted to look at her art on Instagram, yet didn't want to accidently like any of the pictures. He wanted to play it cool and take his time with her.

He felt the urge to do something to let off steam. He found that he wished to enter the magical realm. Taking his key out, he opened a doorway that led him back to his home in Locgarden.

There he showered and changed. He had a whole separate life there. There was no one like Eliza to interest him in the same way. He realised that part of her mystery to him was that she knew nothing of his morph and vampire nature. She only saw him as a man.

James decided he needed to spend the next few days in Locgarden. He would come back to Eliza refreshed, knowing no time had passed since he had sent her the message saying how he had enjoyed her company.

James spent the next few days enjoying the pubs of Locgarden. He had two nights in a row where he drank merrily and enjoyed the company of local acquaintances he knew well in the city.

On the second night, at one in the morning, the hot air and the alcohol finally got to James. He parted company with his friends and decided to wander through the warm city.

The night was full of magic. His vampiric senses could hear people's heartbeats racing as they danced and sang in the bustling bars of the city.

He knew he needed a fix, that sensation that drove him mad with pleasure. He tuned himself into his prowler instincts, as he called upon a victim in his mind.

He had sensed a young girl of only twenty nearby and his powers had linked into her aura, pulling her towards him. The girl was under his spell as she silently obeyed and came forth to the alley, where he waited in the almost pitch dark.

There was just enough light in the alleyway to see her light blonde hair and slender frame. He regarded it for just a moment as he took her into his arms. Sinking his fangs into her neck, he drunk the blood that flowed into his mouth.

He felt all her secrets rush into his mind, all that belonged to her flash before his eyes. He loved it when the blood did trippy things like this to him. He drank deep and slowly from her.

As he felt her heart begin to slow, as thoughts danced in her consciousness of things beyond what was currently happening to her, he felt the nagging sensation of guilt. She was completely under his spell, and would easily fall into death. Yet it had been a long time since he had taken life.

He withdrew from his bite and looked upon the girl. Her eyes were blue and she had freckles on her small face. She looked at him with the blank expression of a victim that has no control over the magic that is overpowering them.

He willed that she would leave him now. He wiped the memory of him feeding upon her easily from her silly little mind. He laughed to himself as she easily walked away, unaware that she had been close to death. Her thoughts had consisted of her boyfriend and obviously daft friends who she enjoyed drinking with in her local pub.

'Silly little mortal girl,' James said, feeling her blood ring hot in his veins.

He was pleased with himself that he hadn't given into temptation and taken her life. Death is such an exciting prospect for a vampire to bring to a mortal.

Vampires enjoy the moment of death so very much. They experience all sorts of pleasure when the human runs dry and their very essence gives the vampire its pure truths, which the person doesn't even know. The blood rush is so sensual and the blood that takes a life away is the sweetest.

James didn't let himself think much more on the girl; he knew that if he overthought it, he would end up willing her to come back to him. He loved the kill, yet hated the guilt it brought him.

He wondered if his mother had been much of a killer. His father hadn't told him much about his late mother.

His father had no idea that James indulged in vampiric activities from time to time, where he fed on mortals in the magical realm.

When James returned to his house in the city of Locgarden, he decided it would be best to sleep off his encounter with the pretty young blonde before returning to London.

He didn't have a job or any obligations in Locgarden. His life there was one of leisure. He had always lived a double life between London and Locgarden.

As a small child, he had attended a private school for supernatural children. It was hidden from the mortals of this realm. Agnes had always picked him up from school when he was little.

He had also attended a high school, which was an expensive private supernatural school for wealthy residents of Locgarden. The city was huge and there was a vast amount of supernatural residents from all sorts of wealth brackets.

His father had always wanted him to pursue some sort of degree in morph magic in this realm. He always stated that one day he would indeed do so.

'What if you're no longer a morph?' – his father's words were always etched in his mind.

Morphs aren't technically morph anymore, once they have children. The power to shapeshift, and wield the magic of nature and the elements, leaves their body as soon as their first child is born.

His father could still enter the magical realm whenever he pleased, yet he chose not to. He was content to leave that world as part of his past.

James did not have the same life as his father. If he was ever to become a father, granted his morph powers would leave his body, yet he would still be an immortal vampire. He would watch those around him grow old and die. Could he bring a son or daughter into the world knowing they too would inherit vampire genes? His morph heritage told him it was the right thing to do, yet he wasn't just morph and these thoughts would eat him up inside at times.

James soon returned back to London, where he got back into the swing of his routine. He mused on calling upon Agnes, but didn't want to tell her about Eliza, as he still felt unsure what her feelings for him were.

He usually found it so easy to connect with women, on at least a superficial level. Yet Eliza was obviously deep and intellectual. That's why she was so interesting to him. There was so much more to her than her beauty.

Chapter Five

James was to visit his father today. He drove up to the flat in Mayfair where his father had always lived. It was a grand property with a white exterior and high windows.

Edgar Daniels greeted his son with a faint yet tired smile. He was a man of sixty-six years, and his face was lined. He looked much like an older version of his very handsome son, except his hair was bald at the top and he was portly.

Edgar sat in his favourite armchair in the living room of the flat. The room held an impressive fireplace with beautiful decorations carved into it. There was a large flat screen TV, which sat opposite Edgar's favourite armchair. Books on philosophy and world history were proudly placed in the many bookcases that sat in the large room.

'Cup of tea?' Edgar asked his son.

'Sure,' James replied.

His father made his way to the kitchen, leaving James to sit on the expensive armchair near to Edgar's favourite chair. James thought to himself how much he had loved this flat growing up.

Edgar's parenting style had been to be stressed. He had always been worried for his son, who he loved dearly. He always stressed the importance that his son become a worthwhile morph. He didn't leave all the training to Agnes, who was around all the time when James was little. Edgar would quiz his son in the history and philosophy of morph culture.

Edgar returned with the tea and placed it on an antique coffee table next to the armchair James was sitting on.

'Good to see you, my boy,' Edgar said, his voice now thin and raspy. 'Now tell me, what's new in your life?'

'Work, mainly. Everything's really good there. I think I'll be promoted soon.'

Edgar waved a dismissive hand at his son's statement. 'Well, it's not like you damn well need the money, yet progressing in work is something that's good. Well done, boy.'

James didn't say that he had met a wonderful woman. He knew that his father wouldn't approve. Edgar would ask if she had any magical lineage. Did she descend from witches' blood or the original psychics who bred with the people of this realm? In other words, was her heritage in any way connected to the magical realm from generations far passed?

James was well aware that Eliza was in no way magical. There wasn't a shred of magic in her aura. His father would only complain about his interest in Eliza, so there was no point bringing it up.

James and his father shared some small talk. They discussed the weather and politics. His father was very concerned with the current affairs of this world. He had distanced himself with the magical realm when James was born, stating he no longer felt the desire to visit often.

For some reason, Edgar was chattier than usual. After the second cup of tea, he began to lament about his deceased wife.

'Your mother was a great beauty; you get your looks from her, I'm sure of it.'

James didn't know what to say and so simply nodded.

'She was not the person I expected to love. Sometimes I would think, *Has she compelled me? Has she enthralled me with powers stronger than my own?* I really do believe that she may have compelled me to love her at the beginning,' Edgar said.

'Dad, we don't have to talk about her, it's not necessary,' James said, knowing how upset the subject of talking about his late wife made Edgar. Stephanie was a subject rarely discussed.

'I know I don't often mention your mother, you know it's painful for me. Boy, I want to show you something. I have kept this from you for long enough. It's time for you to know.'

Edgar motioned for James to follow him into his bedroom. It was the smallest of the bedrooms in the flat. His room was clean and smelled fresh from the weekly visit by the cleaning staff. Edgar's single bed was designed for an old person. There was another of those comfortable armchairs facing another TV that was smaller in size.

Edgar opened the drawer by his bed and brought out a small brown box. He handed it to James, who looked confused.

'When you open this box that I've kept from you for so long, I hope you're not angry with me once you come back from the vision.'

'It's a vision box?' James asked with a gasp, knowing that only a very powerful witch could enchant a box so that one could see visions of the past or the future within it.

'Just open it, my son.'

James nervously opened the box. A flash of white light escaped the box and James was pulled into a vision of the past. He found himself watching his late mother sitting in front of a dressing table in the larger of the flat's bedrooms.

James saw himself in a cot beside her; the new mother was radiant, yet he could feel her energy from the vision box; it was dark and preoccupied with worry.

'Edgar, Edgar!' Stephanie shouted.

'Coming, my love!' shouted her husband, as he entered the bedroom. Edgar put his arms around his wife and kissed her on the cheek. 'How's my lovely wife?'

'I'm fine. Perfectly fine. Go fetch Agnes, will you.'

The vision showed Edgar leaving the room and calling for Agnes. Agnes looked as she always had, like a fat sixty-year-old woman with a joyful face, except here her expression was one of worry.

'Have you told Edgar yet?' Agnes's expression was full of concern.

'Just tell me one thing,' barked Stephanie, 'where did you last see the hunter?!'

'Here in this realm. You need to move quickly. You need to be honest with Edgar about your lifestyle … the feeding. A vampire hunter has caught your scent, so you need to move fast, maybe further than either of the realms, away from Earth and the magical realm. There are witches that can do these things, you know there are.'

'Fine … fine,' said Stephanie with a sneer, obviously very agitated. 'Forget we ever spoke on these matters,' she said, as she used her powers to wipe Agnes's memories of the deadly matters.

'Awww, little baby James is doing well. Going to be an upstanding morph-vampire man, isn't he,' Agnes cooed.

'He'll be the noblest of them all,' said Stephanie with a sigh.

The vision then showed Stephanie instructing Agnes to look after the baby. Stephanie used her key to enter the magical realm. Here she desperately searched for a good witch to help her. Yet the women she encountered were not quite gifted enough.

As she went from one stool to another, she drank in the aura of the witches she spoke with to access if they could do it; if they could take her to a world where the hunter would never reach her – she sensed that the hunter was no longer in London and was resting in Locgarden.

Yet before she could flee and find somewhere private to enter her life back in London, she heard the heavy footsteps of the hunter.

Moments of frantic racing took place. Both women were supernatural beings who ran like the wind.

Yet soon the vampire hunter was upon Stephanie. James couldn't see what he or she looked like in the vision, for their essence was masked. Yet he beheld the fight that took place and how his mother lost the battle.

She was beheaded and her body burnt to cinders. In a dark, abandoned property, she died frightened and frantic. Thoughts of her son James were the last conscious utterances of her mind before she perished.

James found that the vision ended on this image. He was harshly drawn back to the reality of standing in his father's bedroom. Yet he finally knew the truth, the secret of how his mother had died.

Feeling his head spin, he tried his best to compose himself for his father's sake. It was clear from the vision why the vampire hunter had tracked his mother. She was a killer. No vampire hunter in history went after a peaceful vampire who never partook in their hunter's nature.

'She wasn't the mother I wanted for you,' Edgar finally said.

'I … I'll need some time to clear my head,' James stuttered.

'Take all the time you need. I'm sorry I kept this from you for so long. I was afraid it would hurt you if you knew what type of woman your mother really was. The kind that attracts the reapings of a hunter.'

James did his best to talk with his father some more, yet he was deeply shaken. His father didn't know about the fact he fed at times and had indeed killed people in the magical city of Locgarden.

He had never told his father because he was terrified to be disowned. He imagined Agnes would never regard him in the same way again, either, although she was bound to him until he passed the morph blood to a child.

James spent an uncomfortable hour with his father, watching TV and making awkward small talk that was completely off topic from the huge revelation he had just received.

James was glad to go home. He willed himself to compose his thoughts and be calm for just long enough to drive back.

At home, he felt dreadful. Usually, when he didn't feel right in himself, he would enter the magical realm. Yet he couldn't bear to go there right now, knowing his mother had died in Locgarden, looking desperately to escape her fate.

He noted that Eliza had posted a new profile picture on Facebook. She was wearing a little make-up and her slender lips were coloured red. She looked gorgeous, and for a moment it took his mind off the upsetting truths of the day.

I really enjoyed meeting with you. Eliza, I really like you. I was wondering if you would want to go out on a date with me? he quickly typed in her private messages.

As he awaited the reply, he composed himself, thinking how if Eliza would see him as a potential boyfriend, he would change his ways for the time being. No more frolicking with Neava and feeding on young women in Locgarden.

Chapter Six

Eliza was nervous for that first date with James. Not only was it their first date as a potential couple, it was the first date Eliza had been on with another person.

James was coming to Chesham to meet her on this cold Saturday. Eliza had woken hours before she needed to. Her heart beat nervously in her chest as anticipation and self-doubt engulfed her thoughts.

She had been awake since 7 a.m. She hadn't slept well, either. She felt tired and on edge. She looked at herself in the mirror and it was clear that the tiredness showed.

She imagined how James would change his mind after this one date and realise that they had nothing in common.

Jessica knocked on her door; she was the only person Eliza had informed about her date with James.

'Can I come in?' Jessica asked.

'Sure,' Eliza said, sounding tired.

Her sister looked bright and refreshed. She was wearing her work uniform, where she was an assistant manager at Superdrug. 'You look really tired, sis. Why don't you arrange to meet this evening or even tomorrow? James will understand. You don't want to go on a first date exhausted.'

'It's just I feel sick thinking about the date. I don't think I can sleep any more with all the anticipation that I have regarding seeing him.'

Jessica made a sad face. 'You're a beautiful girl. I know our mum's not the best woman in the world to instil self-esteem, but you are truly pretty. You're also kind and incredibly smart, as well as talented.'

'You're the apple of Mum's eye and she sees me as the runt of the litter.'

'It's because I'm more like her, I guess. I think she feels because I look like her when she was young, that the fact that I'm quite an outgoing person is a reflection on her. She's stupid not to value your lovely quiet nature. I know she loves you very much.'

'I love her, too. Although she does my head in at times,' Eliza said with a laugh.

'Text James. Rearrange the date and get some sleep. I need to be at work in half an hour, so I better walk into town.'

'Thanks, sis,' Eliza said, as she watched her sister leave her bedroom.

Eliza took her sister's advice and arranged that they meet much later. James called her up and he sounded perfectly fine with a change in the time.

Eliza did her best to compose herself. She tried hard to throw away her worries and not experience them anymore, for now at least.

She crawled into bed feeling sluggish and drained. Turning off the little lamp next to her bed, she weakly drifted off into sleep.

In her dreams, she dreamt that a man was following her through a ball of colour. It led into a world beyond a world of shapes and figures she couldn't make out. There was a sense of otherworldly magic in the air.

Eliza awoke refreshed, forgetting the dream. She showered and got ready to meet James.

As she got ready, she straightened her hair and applied a bright red lipstick. She wore eyeliner and more make-up than she usually applied. She wore a pretty brown dress with polka dots. Wearing small heels and a sophisticated perfume, she felt this was the best she could do.

*****

When James arrived in Chesham, he waited to meet Eliza at the station, where he had parked his car. He saw he was a few minutes early when he checked his phone. He waited for ten minutes before he saw her walking up the road to the station.

She was wearing a dark green coat and heels, and her hair was longer and straight, unlike its usual wavy curls. He smiled seeing her, drinking in that rich and mysterious aura. As she walked closer, the aura became stronger, as though it was dancing around all his senses. Exciting him and seducing him to this amazing woman who he found so interesting.

'You do look lovely,' James said, as they met. He leaned in lightly to kiss her on the cheek and felt her shake ever so slightly.

It was eight in the evening. The two went to an Indian restaurant called the Ragestan. It was a tiny walk from the station. As they walked together, James enquired about her day.

'Yes, perfectly fine, thank you,' she replied.

James could tell from her aura that she felt anxious and was feeling self-doubt. Something a normal man wouldn't ever be able to read off her.

They ordered starters and drinks. Eliza did not order any alcohol and had a coke.

'Would you like to see a movie sometime next week?' he asked, making sure she was clear that he was indeed very interested in her.

She blushed deeply at the question. 'Yes, why not,' she replied.

James wanted to get to know more about Eliza. He asked her if she had studied art before university. He already knew both her degrees were in Fine Arts.

'Oh, yes. I studied Fine Arts at Amersham College. It's just the next town from us and my dad would always drive me there. Jessica went there as well, but she studied Fashion Design and was in the year below me, as she's a year younger than me. We both did our BTECs there.'

James told her that Bradley really liked Jessica. He said he was lucky that he had met someone that night that he also liked.

'I like you as well,' she stuttered.

Their food arrived; they had both ordered vegetable samosas, as Eliza had recommended them. James copied her and also ordered vegetable biryani for his main dish.

He was careful not to drink too much, even though his powers meant he could brush off the influence of alcohol upon himself. He knew Eliza wasn't impressed by men who drank much; it was something he could read off her.

The awkwardness of the night slipped away as they talked about art, family and friends. They were getting to know each other and it was magical.

James was careful not to focus on her slender figure in that polka dot dress and how elegant and appealing he found her body. He was also careful not to linger for too long on her emerald green eyes, knowing he would be entranced. He would also see her inner secrets, unlike normal men, and his morph gifts would reveal secrets he yearned to wait for and find in their natural time.

He was smitten with Eliza. By the time they had finished the meal, it was 10 p.m. He wanted to ask her to go to a pub for a bit, but could still feel a great sense of shyness and self-doubt radiating from her.

Feeling aware that her insecurities were crippling, he broke his own rule of plan; using his morph gifts, he eased the doubt from her thoughts just long enough that he could passionately kiss her on the lips.

Her body was pressed against his and it was clear that she could feel his desire for her. She was a good kisser for someone who had never kissed. It was a secret her body sang deeply and one that made his heart smile.

James drove her back to her house, where he kissed her simply on the cheek once more.

'Eliza, I really like you. I can't wait to go to the cinema with you next week. Let me know what film you want to see.'

'I had a great time. I look forward to seeing you again soon.'

Seeing that she was in her house, James drove off. He felt excited about his first official date with Eliza Barnet.

Chapter Seven

James had always lived a double life. Agnes had taught him how to use the magical key from a young age. It led to the family home in Locgarden. James had always loved how he could take weeks away from responsibilities in his life and then simply return at his will, knowing no time had passed since he had left.

From a young age, he had double the education requirements of his peers. He attended private education in Mayfair, and this is how he met Bradley in middle school. They were both wealthy boys from successful families.

Yet James also attended the private educational institutes in Locgarden, which were tailored for students with supernatural qualities. Everyone from witches to psychics attended the school. The school was cloaked in ancient magic, which meant the world around it just believed it to be an exclusive and expensive school.

None of the children could be said to look magical from just viewing them. In reality, witches don't have green skin or wear big hats. In fact, they are often very fashion-conscious and as diverse as any other group. No one could tell someone was a witch just from looking at them. You would have to be supernatural yourself to be able to feel the magic that radiated off them.

If a normal person spoke a witch's spells aloud, nothing would happen, as they wouldn't have the power in them to ignite the magic that surrounded this realm.

Morphs are very different from witches; not only can they shapeshift, their magic isn't ignited from spells, but rather from emotions and feelings of the world around them.

During primary school, there was an air of innocence in the children of Locgarden's School for the Supernatural. Vampires got on with werewolves, witches played with morphs. The school grounds for the primary school were separated, as was the location for the middle and high school.

It was believed that each state of a supernatural being's life should be treasured and taken slowly.

James acquired many friends during his time at the School for the Supernatural; yet no one was quite like his friend Maggie, who influenced him so greatly.

Maggie was a full-blooded vampire. Her family were loving and the sorts that would never dream of partaking in the 'dark' nature of a vampire's thirst.

There tended to be two sorts of vampire – firstly, there were those who believed they were blessed to be immortal and were thankful for the gifts this could bestow, such as seeing the worlds change so much. These vampires weren't the threatening ones that killed people.

The 'dark vampire' was a term to describe a vampire that lets its bloodlust control it and who would kill without guilt. They were regarded badly by the other vampires and were also feared, because they attracted vampire hunters. Like the one James now knew had killed his own mother.

James had met Maggie in primary school and they had connected instantly over the fact they were both vampires. She was interested in his morph side but always stated being vampire was superior.

She was a mischievous girl even when they were little. She would steal other students' lunch meals from their lockers, eat only the candy and throw away the sandwiches and fruit.

She could be a tad of a bully at times and would make rude comments about students she regarded as 'un-pretty'. James ignored her mean traits growing up because she was so exciting. She made him feel alive when after school they would go on adventures.

They would tease psychics with false questions, or go on a magic carpet through the city. Things like that had made attending the magical school so exciting.

Yet it was in middle school when James turned eleven that Maggie's influence over him became darker. She brought in blood in a bottle. James had never drank blood, even though his body often thought about it and the idea of it excited him in a way he knew was wrong and evil.

Maggie convinced him to drink the human blood, stating no person had been harmed in the acquisition of it. James remembered the intoxication and loss of care in those moments. He could still remember how it had made him feel on top of the world. How he had been rude in class that day when he had his final lesson.

Maggie left it for a while but this event happened again. It was in his final year of middle school that James began to regularly drink blood with Maggie.

The act changed the way he saw himself. It made him feel more connected with his mother's heritage and in tune with what it meant to be an immortal vampire.

In his school on Earth, the blood drinking would sometimes affect his personality. It wasn't like he took blood in that reality, yet the effects didn't wear off easily. He lost interest in his school work. Luckily, he managed to maintain his friendship with Bradley, who although concerned for him, understood that people change.

James's studies picked up and he eventually swam through high school in London. Both he and Bradley got top grades in their GCSEs thanks to their numerous tutors and the excellent school that they attended.

One of the effects of drinking human blood if you are a vampire is that your memory becomes sharper. So, this was also aiding him in his achievements. In his life in Locgarden, he took exams in magic and folklore for vampires and morphs. He wrote essays about the history of both creatures and passed well.

His father was proud of him, yet he did not realise that by now, not only was he drinking bottled blood with Maggie, they were also feeding together.

There are dark places in Locgarden that belong to the likes of the dark vampires. They have been blessed by evil witches to allow those vampires to have endless supplies of mortals in farms that are outside of the dimension of the magical realm.

Neither Maggie nor James had a key for these 'kitchens', as they were described. Yet for the right money, they could pay to enjoy the experience of feeding on one of these humans bred for the vampires' consumption.

They entered the realm, which was huge yet the owners of the specific club had decorated it in purples and black. In a booth, a woman was brought for them who couldn't speak and simply made squeaks and sounds like a monkey.

Maggie and James devoured her together. James was sixteen years old and it was the first person he had murdered. He experienced images of a woman in a cell all her life with no interaction with other people and no mental stimulation. She had been drugged to numb any fear or aggression. James knew he should feel sorry for her, but at the time the buzz of killing a mortal was too exciting for him. It felt too good and he didn't want the sensation to end.

Throughout his post-secondary school education in Locgarden and the private sixth form on Earth, he would feed in the magical realm with Maggie.

Maggie became his first girlfriend and someone who changed the path of his life forever. He didn't love Maggie. He used her as a way to explore his own dark nature. He had surely wanted this, or else he would have stopped partaking in such acts.

When he went to university at the London School of Economics and didn't also study in Locgarden anymore for a degree in a supernatural field, he didn't see Maggie as often.

Maggie went on to study and they soon broke up. She had stated she wanted to try new things.

Without Maggie's influence, James expected to stop hunting and killing. Yet he didn't. Although it wasn't as frequent, it still happened. He was the type of vampire his mother had been. He was a dark vampire and no amount of guilt would stop him from doing what felt so good to him.

Chapter Eight

Eliza was in awe that she had met someone like James. She had secretly never expected to experience romance, a feeling she hadn't told anyone she possessed.

Eliza was preparing for her second date with James. She wore a plain black pencil dress and flat shoes. The pencil dress outlined her perfectly slender body that was long and elegant.

Eliza's curly brown hair was freshly washed. She smelled of her Dior perfume, which was her signature scent. She applied a red lipstick to her lips.

As she travelled to London, where James was to meet her to attend an art gallery, she felt nervous. She saw herself as plain in comparison to his model-esque appearance.

When James arrived outside the art gallery, he was dressed casually yet he looked as though his clothes were designer. His hair looked carefree and his strong features were beautiful in the sunlight.

'It's good to see you again,' James said, kissing her on the mouth, which took her by surprise.

She felt her heart flutter as she kissed him back. It felt like time stood still as they kissed. A moment of passion that she wasn't used to. Something alien to her.

They walked through the art gallery. It was filled with modern art. The gallery was showing amazing artists of present times who had become successful in the art world.

'That could be your work up there one day.'

'Oh, I couldn't dream of it,' Eliza said, brushing the compliment away.

As they walked through the gallery, they held hands from time to time. It was something so simple yet very sensual to Eliza.

They spent two hours in the gallery looking at the works of art. After this, they walked to a nearby restaurant that James had been recommended.

Eliza felt shy sitting opposite him in the restaurant. His grey jumper looked so sexy on his finely carved shoulders.

James talked about himself, telling her what his work was like. He confessed that his father had bought him his flat and how he simply worked for a sense of independence.

'It's my way of feeling successful for my own achievements, you know,' he said.

The restaurant was posh. They ate baked fish and finely cooked vegetables. Eliza had a small glass of wine, which ever so slightly eased her nerves, because she very rarely drank any alcohol at all.

The conversation was light yet also revealing into who each of them were. Eliza was surprised how much she clicked with James. Maybe it was because he seemed so attentive to her interests and aspirations for life.

She told him how she wanted to continue her studies in Fine Arts for a PhD. She simply loved being at university; it was the collective energy of a university that she adored.

'It's impressive meeting a girl who wants a PhD,' James said, as he looked lovingly into her eyes.

The date was magical. When it ended and Eliza was back on the train on her way home to Chesham, she felt the journey swim by. Her thoughts dreamily focused on James and how she so hoped they would continue to see each other.

*****

Time flew by. Eliza and James began to meet twice a week for dates over the next month. They found they enjoyed each other's sense of humour and were obviously attracted to one another.

James bought Eliza a silver heart pendant after they had been seeing one another for a month. He confessed that the necklace was a token of his affection for Eliza.

Eliza was scared to truly analyse her feelings for James. She kept them to herself and had only talked with her sister Jessica about how she was dating him. Her parents had no idea that Eliza had a boyfriend.

*****

The dates were magical affairs, where Eliza felt like a princess with James. She felt carefree when he talked confidently. How she loved his smell and the warmth of his kisses.

The dates became more passionate each time, so that it was inevitable that they would eventually end up at his flat.

She felt too nervous to comment on how nice the property was as they stepped into the white-walled flat. She had drank a little wine that evening and had kissed James passionately on and off during the night.

Now, as they entered his large bedroom, she felt her heart flutter. She looked into his chocolate eyes and felt heat, such passion radiated from him.

'I want you,' he said, breathing hard.

As she nervously undressed, he was confident and poised in comparison. How she loved his smell and the warmth of his kisses.

Did he realise that Eliza was a virgin? It wasn't something they had talked about.

Yet as she lay down naked on the bed and he crawled on top of her like an excited animal, they entered into sexual activity. There was touching and urges to be expressed.

Eliza was glad of the wine, which allowed the experience to soften as he made love gently yet urgently to her.

She wanted every inch of him and to truly feel his body inside her and around her. She was falling for this man, a love she did her best not to overanalyse.

When they had finished making love, they lay together in the bed. Tiredness overtook James and Eliza, who slept together in harmony.

'I adore you' were the last words Eliza heard before a strange sense of tiredness took her body, which seemed to be roused from James himself. It was a weird feeling that she didn't attribute to the supernatural, knowing nothing of James's secret identity as half-morph, half-vampire.

Chapter Nine

James woke to find Eliza sleeping in the tiredness which he roused in her. She looked beautifully peaceful. He would come back to her in moments, before she would ever wake.

Stepping into his bathroom, he took out his invisible key, which only those belonging to the magical realm could see. He opened the doorway to the magical realm, finding himself in his familiar house in Locgarden.

Here it was morning, as it was on Earth. The sky was pink and bright. As James looked out of his window he smiled, thinking to himself about the day he would have before he came back to sleeping Eliza.

He showered in his house, washing with spiced soaps that were very distinctive of the city's fragrances. He enjoyed the sensation of hot water on his aroused body. How he had enjoyed being with Eliza, whom he cherished. She was a beauty and so smart, which was something he found so sexy about her.

After showering, he dried himself off and dressed in the silk fashions of the city. Colouring himself in purple, loose-fitting trousers and a light pink shirt. His shoulder-length brown hair dried naturally as he left for town.

In town, he walked through Locgarden, thinking about what he wanted from this city. How he craved the glorious night and how he would hunt.

He thought about the day weaning to an end as he drank mint tea in a café, sitting outside and watching the mortals and witches pass him by.

He returned home after a while, where he made himself busy writing in a journal. Here in his home at Locgarden, he freely wrote about his vampiric nature in the journal. How he knew his father would be disappointed to know he hunted, yet he was too giddy from Eliza to care. His needs were selfish tonight.

When the sun set, he ventured out again. Taking his time, he went deep into the city, far from his home. Here there was poverty amongst superstitious and uneducated mortals.

The literacy levels of the mortals of this part of the city was very low. Education was missed by them and many of these humans could only recite passages of religious books from oral memory.

James called his victim from deep inside the young boy's inner being. He pulled and gently broke his will without an itty bit of effort. From the shadows, James waited as the young boy of seventeen walked slowly in a daze. He wasn't near his home and didn't understand where he was walking to.

The young boy's will had been dulled to nothing, so he felt not a care in the world as he encountered James. James touched his neck, observing the rags that he wore and the bright orange colour of his hair.

James sunk his teeth into the teenager's neck, drinking quietly and urgently. Wanting to know the secrets that the boy held.

As his heartbeat slowed with every wave of weakness that James induced in him, more of his life story was revealed. His thoughts and feelings sang into James's body as he greedily induced death in the boy.

As the teenager died at James's will, he put the boy's body down on the floor in the darkened corner where he had been feeding.

Here he slowly and quietly made his way away from the boy and the scene of darkness, feeling the tale of who the boy was continue to unravel in his mind as the blood was fully appreciated by his body.

The teenager's name had been Jerico; he had lived with his four siblings and parents. None of them could read or write, and they lived working on farming and doing tasks for the 'wise women' who they had suspicions were witches.

Jerico would be missed greatly by his family. James knew this but his vampiric pleasure outweighed any cares he now had for the people of Locgarden.

He was becoming a colder man with every kill, only holding sympathy for his loved ones on Earth. He no longer cared about the humans who he fed on. The guilt was less pronounced each time.

He enjoyed the night as he made his way back to his home in Locgarden. He showered once again but this time the water was cold, to shake off the heat of his body warm from the kill.

He knew he must not return to Eliza just yet. So, he slept in his bed in Locgarden. When he awoke, he spent several days in the city, simply reading and enjoying quiet meals alone.

When he was ready to return to the bed he had left on Earth, he found Eliza in peaceful sleep. He waited for her to wake, her green eyes fluttering, and she smiled with the intelligence in her expression that he adored.

'Morning, beautiful,' he said.

She kissed him sweetly on the mouth, replying, 'Morning.'

They had breakfast together. They ate cheese bagels and drank tea. Eliza was shy that morning and James found it beautifully endearing.

They made love again in the afternoon and she slept another night at his flat. He enjoyed the uninterrupted pleasure of her sleeping in his bed.

Chapter Ten

Eliza was excited about going to Paris. Not only was she going with James, but also her sister and Bradley. The two couples had a double date a while back where they went to Nando's together after one of Eliza's art exhibitions.

Yet going abroad with her boyfriend was a big step for Eliza. The couple were now getting comfortable with intimacy. It seemed everything was falling into place.

Eliza was too scared to mention words of love, but often expressed how fond she was of James to him. He would tell her how he loved and adored her, which made her heart flutter.

As the two couples travelled by first class on a ferry to Paris, they talked about little things.

'I'm so proud of Eliza, she's nearly finished her Master's degree,' Jessica said.

'Yes, my girl is rather clever,' James said with a smile.

'I think we should toast to new beginnings,' Bradley said, beaming. 'How several months ago both us lads met the most amazing girls.'

Everyone smiled at the remark. 'I've got something important to announce, actually. I hope I don't seem like a love-struck idiot, but I have to ask … I have to know,' Bradley said, with hope in his eyes. 'Jessica, I've never met anyone so lovely as you and someone whom I connect so well with.'

'Bradley,' Jessica said, blushing.

'I'd like to know if you would do me the honour of being my wife?' Bradley asked, revealing a beautiful ring in front of the group.

'Yes, Bradley, of course I will,' Jessica said, as she kissed him and accepted the ring.

The ring was a delicate object featuring a pretty heart-shaped diamond. It was a beautiful engagement ring, which sat well on Jessica's dainty hands.

When the couples got to Paris, they celebrated by dining in a luxurious French restaurant, where they had crisp white wine and fine food.

When the two couples got to their hotel in the centre of Paris, Eliza was tired. She was glad to sleep that night in the comfort of James's arms, the smell of his fresh scent mixing with the air around her.

She was so pleased that Bradley and Jessica were to be married. She wondered what their wedding would be like.

*****

As the sunlight of a warm day in Paris gently illuminated the hotel room, Eliza awoke to feelings of peacefulness. James looked so at ease in the bed next to her, sleeping soundly.

She got up and looked at her phone. Her mum had texted her regarding her excitement about Jessica's news. Her mum didn't even know that Eliza was in a relationship with James.

Eliza guessed she had feared her mother's overenthusiastic reaction, which she predicted would put pressure on her. She vowed to herself that she would let her mother know she was dating James once they got home from Paris.

James stirred in the bed, 'Should we get up soon?'

'There's no rush, it's still early,' Eliza replied, as she put her phone down on the bedside table.

James found effective uses for time that they had together before they ventured out into the city.

Eliza and James spent a day alone in the city together. They dined in a fine restaurant, where they talked about the little things that fill up a couple's time together. Little snippets of small talk that seem magical when with the right person.

They went up the Eiffel Tower, where the heights slightly freaked out Eliza, who was glad to leave the attraction and take a photo from the safety of the ground below.

'Oh, how I love you,' James said, as they walked back to the hotel on the crisp evening.

'And I you,' Eliza replied nervously, never before expressing such emotions so clearly to him.

'I never want to lose you. Eliza, you are simply the very best thing that has ever happened to me.'

*****

James was thankful to hear Eliza express feelings of love. He felt those emotions in her aura, deep and clear as day. He adored every strand of hair on her head. She was his everything.

As they enjoyed one final day in Paris with Bradley and Jessica, they caught an artsy film together. The two men had taken French in school, along with Spanish, yet neither of them expressed how they could understand the dialogue without the subtitles.

The film was a sad tale of a young teenage girl falling pregnant and keeping a baby that completely changed the course of her life. She began to resent the child as it grew older and began to resemble the father who had left her when she was only seventeen.

'What a wonderful film,' Eliza said, beaming, as they walked out of the quaint little cinema.

'Yes, it really was a good movie,' Bradley said. 'We should start packing for the ferry tomorrow. I think we should all do this again sometime, just go away somewhere nice.'

'Well, we've a wedding to plan first,' said Jessica with a laugh.

'Of course we do!' Bradley said. 'What a wedding it will be, at that.'

Chapter Eleven

When Eliza got back to her room, she was so glad to get changed into her Disney pyjamas. With freshly washed hair and not a trace of make-up, she felt good. Being with James and having his love had changed the way she saw herself. She had always secretly regarded herself as an ugly duckling in comparison to Jessica. It wasn't a feeling she minded or resented in any way, but her truth was changing. Now, when she looked in the mirror, she saw the beauty that James must see when he looked at her.

Her mother knocked on her door. 'Eliza?' she enquired.

'Come in, Mum,' Eliza said, as she sat on the bed.

'Great news about Jessica. She's finally gone and got a ring on her finger,' Moreen said, beaming.

'Yes. Bradley is really great. He's a wonderful match for Jessica.'

'And rich. Stinking rich!' Moreen almost shouted.

Eliza couldn't help but laugh at her mother's outburst. 'Mum, there's something I should tell you.'

'What?'

'I'm also in a relationship.'

'You are?' Moreen asked, raising a questioning eyebrow at her daughter.

'Yes, I've been seeing Bradley's best friend. His name's James Daniels.'

'Oh, oh …' Moreen said, making a strange face. 'Jessica told me about him. She said he was arrogant and stuffy, so he's your boyfriend?'

'Yes, Mum, and he's not arrogant once you get to know him.'

'Is this new?'

'No, Mum. It's been going on for several months now. I just wanted to keep it private.'

'I see,' her mother said.

Eliza continued to talk to her mother about James. Her mother quizzed her as to whether she thought she would be marrying him anytime soon. Eliza said she didn't like to overanalyse what might lie in store in the future and brushed off questions about the nature of marriage.

'Well, at least he's rich and good-looking,' Moreen said, after Eliza showed her a picture of him. 'Well, I've had about as much news as I can take for the evening. Come down and watch *Britain's Got Talent* with us?'

'I've got essays to write. But I'll come down later for some tea,' Eliza said.

'Oh, you and your studying. Well, you are missing out with regards to the TV. See you later when you're done working,' Moreen said, leaving Eliza in her room.

*****

James was in a very happy place in his life. His love for Eliza was warming his heart and making him feel truly connected to this world. He simply adored her.

Yet his life in the magical realm was equally enjoyed. Knowing not a stitch in time had passed since he had delved into mysteries unknown to the mortals of the Earthly reality he also called home.

As he entered his home in Locgarden – a city famous for its shady witches, who weren't to be trusted – James felt a great sense of well-being.

He had recently arranged to meet with his old school friend Maggie. She was the vampire who had given him his path in Locgarden. A secret identity as a hunter, which he had hidden away from his father and Agnes.

There was a time in their late teens when they had been heated lovers, yet their sexual passion had never equated to romantic love. It had been a relationship of attraction and friendship rooted in the fact that they were both vampiric and had the bloodlust of their species.

When Maggie arrived at his home, she was wearing a brown dress and black boots. Her long blonde hair was straight and her make-up was barely noticeable.

She hugged James lightly as she entered the house. She smelt of a fresh perfume.

'You look good … as always,' Maggie said.

'It's been a long time,' James replied.

'I've missed my old hunting buddy,' Maggie said, sitting herself down on the multi-coloured sofa.

'How are things? Are you still working on your Master's in vampiric history?'

'James! I finished that two years ago. Do keep up,' she said, smiling. 'It was great though, learning about who we are and how our race has held power in secret ways throughout the history of the realm.'

'It sounds truly fascinating.'

'You're spending more time on the Earthly realm, aren't you. I see you have a job there and a girlfriend, which you talk about. You only seem to hunt in the realm and pay flighting visits of late.'

'I spend weeks on end here in between work, yet you're right, my life is on the Earthly realm, yet the realm is still my home, too. I could never hunt on Earth, for one thing.'

Maggie's eyes lit up. 'I want to introduce you to someone, later tonight. Remember those "kitchens" in hidden portals, which we used to visit during our teens? Well, you know, the legislations behind vampiric law have made them illegal in

Locgarden, yet there are powerful witches that cloak the doorways to these places.'

'There's plenty a town and city where these things aren't illegal, so why break the law?'

'Oh, you know the penalty's a slap on the wrist, isn't it. What's the harm in living on the wild side?'

James shook his head and laughed lightly. 'So, you want to introduce me to one of these witches then?'

*****

The night was dark when Maggie and James walked through the witches' market. Many of the stools were closed for the night, yet a little wooden stool with a beautiful dark-skinned woman was where the witch in question sat.

She had beautiful curly hair and bright large eyes. Her figure was slender, yet her curves were visible in the black dress that clung to her figure.

'Brandy?' Maggie asked.

The witch looked up and her bright eyes narrowed as she smiled. 'If it isn't my old friend Maggie.'

'It's been a while,' Maggie said with a grin.

'Yeah, you've been off travelling the realm. I know. I know … who's this handsome chap you've brought with ya? I can sense the morph blood in him.'

'This is James. He's a close friend.'

Brandy motioned for the two of them to follow her as she put a closed sign on her wooden stool. They followed in silence as she walked to her flat in the witches' market.

James could sense the dark energy that resonated off Brandy. She had a wicked soul but perhaps he did as well. After all, he was following her into a hidden place where he could feed on innocent humans bred for vampiric consumption. OK, so they were not able to speak any language or know much about anything due to the drugs they were given, yet surely it was still evil.

They entered Brandy's little flat, which was on the third floor of an old yellowed block. Her home was small and full of potions and ritualistic effigies upon the walls. The property had an evil, spooky vibe, as though spirits were lingering and haunting Brandy; not that she cared, for these helpless, angry spirits could do her no harm.

'You'll be wanting to visit the kitchen again, won't you, Maggie?'

'Well, of course I will. As will my friend.'

'Costs more to bring … a friend,' Brandy said.

'Yes, I'm aware of the prices.'

'You see, there was a time when these sorts of shenanigans were legal here in Locgarden, but times change. Political ideologies sway with the people's … or in the case of the law … vampires' ideologies. Not everyone's as enlightened to the needs of your kind as the two of you.'

'They're suppressed!' snapped Maggie.

'I'll be fetching you your key now,' Brandy said, taking the red glowing key out of a little black box displaying incantations in the ancient language of magical practice.

She handed the key to Maggie. 'Enjoy your trip,' Brandy said, as she sat down on a red chair. 'I just need the money before you can take that special ride.'

Maggie handed Brandy her bank card. The witch got out her mobile phone and made the payment go through, 'Well, that's the best two thousand bucks you've spent in a while, I'd expect.'

'See you later,' Maggie said, as she grabbed James's hand.

'Laters,' Brandy said, as she waved a hand.

The magic in the key was ignited. James and Maggie blacked out of the reality in Locgarden, where they were standing in Brandy's flat.

In this temporary state, they entered a place cloaked by evil magic for the consumption and money of vampires. They were in the infamous Kitchen club of Locgarden.

'Welcome to the Kitchen,' said a pretty vampire, who looked as though she was in her late teens. 'Have you been here before?'

'Yeah … well, we used to be regulars a while back,' Maggie said, referring to their teenage years.

'The system's just loading with your order from your witch Brandy. She's got good rates, I must say, from what I've been told by customers I've dealt with,' the teenager said, who had shoulder-length brown hair and was wearing a white dress.

The brunette vampire led them to their booth once their order had loaded. The Kitchen hadn't changed much since they were teenagers. It was still painted purple and had all those chairs where a sexy burlesque vampire act could always be seen being performed.

In the booths, things were not much different, either. For old times' sake, Maggie insisted that they take a double booth.

There in the booth were two tablet screens on the wall, where the two vampire friends could choose the victim they wanted off the menu.

'It's so exciting to be back,' Maggie said, as she swiped through the tablet menu.

'Good old times,' James replied, feeling a mix of guilt and anticipation from the act he was about to enter into.

Maggie selected a victim. A young woman with her hair shaved off and wearing a white slip was inserted into the booth. She looked up at Maggie with a drugged-up gaze and clearly had no idea what was going on.

James could sense the language-less thoughts that came from the woman, and how she knew nothing of nothing. A lifetime of drugs, food and sleep. She was a creation of the Kitchen, who knew nothing of the outside world of Locgarden or the realm beyond the grand city.

As Maggie slowly bit into the neck of the woman, James's hunger stirred as the scent of her fresh blood mixed with the air.

He couldn't reject his friend's offer to feed. She had paid a lot of money for him to enjoy a human life. His guilt was washed away in the lust of the kill, as he selected a random person to come into the booth.

The woman that came out had long brown hair, longer than Eliza's hair, and that was the only feature of hers that reminded him of his love; yet the feelings of guilt were overwhelming once again. What would Eliza think if she knew he was a vampire-morph man? She knew nothing of his secret life.

Maggie pushed the girl towards him and he bowed down to his lust for blood as he delved into her arm and drank. The blood sang a song of curiosity beyond words and thoughts that were in flashes of moods and colours.

His pity for the human before him was washed away as he consumed every ounce of her, feeding into the precious nectar that filled him with ecstasy.

When it was over, both Maggie and James were in a stupor. They stumbled together out of their booth, leaving the dead bodies remaining inside.

The brunette vampire greeted them with a bright, carefree smile. 'We hope you've enjoyed your stay at the Kitchen. Do you want to have any tea and coffee before you fade back?'

'Coffee sounds good,' Maggie slurred.

James nodded his head as they sprawled down into two waiting chairs. A blonde vampire danced burlesque on the stage nearby. She was wearing a blue corset and stockings.

The brunette in the white dress quickly arrived with their coffees. Only vampires worked in this establishment.

'I feel so good,' Maggie mumbled, as she sipped her hot coffee.

James thought of Eliza and her curly brown hair. He imagined the horror that would show in her eyes if only she knew. Yet what did it matter? She was innocent to this world where James had another identity. Unless they were to be bound together for all time, there was no reason why Eliza would ever need to know of this world.

As the buzz began to wear off and Maggie finished her complimentary coffee, they began to black back out of the illegal portal.

They were now back in Brandy's flat. The witch winked at them as she got up from her chair.

'See you again soon,' Brandy said, as she showed them to the door.

Maggie linked arms with James as they walked home. They talked on many things that night. Mostly reminiscing about their teenage years in high school. Maggie talked about how they had grown apart as they had taken on different life paths. She expressed how she missed the carefree adventures where they had fed like this at the Kitchen so many times before in their youth.

When the night was over, Maggie made her way back to her family home in Locgarden, and James sat alone in his house.

He knew she had been pissed off with him for not enjoying the moment as much as they used to when they were young. He had loved and hated it at the very same time.

He couldn't go back to Earth anytime soon; he was hungry for more human blood. He could feed in Locgarden, yet he knew it wasn't legal and nor was it safe.

He had Brandy's number and he knew in his heart that he would visit her tomorrow. Money wasn't an object for him in Locgarden, either. He had currency aplenty! He would feed and enjoy his dark nature until the beast inside of him was full to the brim.

Chapter Twelve

James loved the time that slowly passed by in Locgarden. He needed to explore his dark side and put all his guilt away.

He would make his way to Brandy's stool in the witches' district, where her evil eyes would light up.

'Come back for some more of that good stuff?' she asked, as she ushered him to follow her back to her flat.

The little apartment full of spells was where the evil magic took place. Brandy sat down on a chair, bringing up her mobile phone; ready to take payment for the dreadful and dark place that was the Kitchen.

As James pulled out his bank card, he felt the excitement he experienced each time he entered this place. Knowing it was frowned upon by the general population of Locgarden, who had voted for a consensus where vampires would not feed on human life in such a manner.

Yet the laws varied from city to city in the realm. It was a mere penalty of money that James would have to pay if caught. The vampires looked after their own.

'Have a good trip,' Brandy said, in a tone that held dark amusement.

Brandy cast the spell that opened the portal into the Kitchen. James stepped in and found himself in the modern club, where the magic happened.

The purple décor of the Kitchen felt like a second home to James; he had been visiting this place so much lately.

'You again; you like this place, don't you,' said the brunette vampire host; she had a pear-shaped body that was slender in all the right places.

'I like it here,' James admitted.

'Do you want a drink while we prepare your booth?'

'No, thank you, I'll just wait,' James replied.

James sat and waited on a comfortable chair while his booth was prepared. Anticipation and excitement danced through every atom of his body.

When a fresh booth was ready, James quickly slipped inside, hungrily looking at the menu on the screen before him. He took a moment to compose himself, feeling his heart beat frantically at the excitement he was experiencing.

As he browsed the menu, he noticed it had been updated. There were pictures of the potential victims. He only ever chose to enjoy one human at a time, loving how the person's mind and essence lingered over him for days after the event.

A beautiful woman with thick curly hair and big eyes took his fancy. The menu said she was nineteen. She would have lived her whole existence in the Kitchen's magical warehouses, drugged up for this moment, unable to speak a word of English.

Yet even though these victims weren't vocal like the humans he sometimes killed in Locgarden, they were full of that amazing vitality and essence that could never be stripped from a victim.

As the teenager dropped down into the booth, James gently took her in his arms. She smelt of the fresh perfume that he had chosen when ordering her on the menu. He liked his victims to smell good.

She simply looked at him, staring into his eyes without any sort of questioning. It was enough for James to be driven mad with hunger as he delved deep into her bloodstream.

Images of thoughts unformed by words and emotions not truly understood by the girl flooded through James's mind. He took every ounce of her, and when she died, he felt such a great sense of exhilaration.

He left the booth and said farewell to the brown-haired waitress. As he re-entered Brandy's flat, he felt alive and ready to do anything that this wonderful city could grace him with. Tonight, he would fly high on a magic carpet and later he may morph into a wolf.

Each life he took led him further into his vampire nature. He was intoxicated by the blood when it swam over him, making him feel invincible.

He needed this time to simply be. He wanted the gap between his life on Earth, which felt as though it was his true destiny. He felt as though he was more of a man with a destiny in Eliza's arms, yet exploring being a vampire was so very powerful.

He spent the year in the arms of Neava. The blue-haired beauty would wake up in his arms each morning without any look of judgement in those carefree eyes. He knew how she loved him. He could feel the emotions of love bleeding from her aura.

Tonight was the same. He had fed well on the teenager and indeed he had for a short while morphed into a wolf, rolling around on the spare bed and wishing to run free in the forests beyond the city.

When it was Neava who he called upon, there was no judgement for his evil deeds. She knew of his identity as a man who was part-morph and part-vampire. Perhaps that's why she loved him.

******

Neava loved James. This was apparent in the little gestures she made, such as how she would describe him as her 'beautiful one'. It was obvious from the simple fact of the matter that she had willingly given her life over to be owned by James.

Other mortal women in her life had either distanced themselves from Neava or completely cut ties. She didn't care. She had the protection of a healthy vampire and a comfortable house of her own to live in. Surely she needed nothing more in life.

Their sex together was passionate and full of longing. The type of longing experienced when two beautiful people are utterly in lust, which is something superficial.

When she had moved away, her mother had asked her, 'Neava, won't you miss the joys of being a normal girl?'

Neava brushed such thoughts out of her mind most of the time. She had a man who would visit her often in this realm, and although she knew he loved someone else – a woman on Earth – he had never admitted it to her.

'Neava, my beautiful blue-haired goddess,' cooed James.

'Oh, right here? Right now?' begged Neava, looking into James's deep brown eyes.

As they passionately made love, they kissed violently, touching and caressing each other's bodies. James's touch was harsh yet so pleasurable. He entered her with great urgency, and when it was over, they lay together in his bed.

Neava watched as James slept. She thought about what her mum had said, about how having a normal life would have been good for her. Her mum rarely spoke to her now and had a disappointed look in her eyes whenever she did. A kept woman was basically another word for a rich prostitute. Owned by someone of high financial status. Her mother had no idea that James was supernatural.

At the University of Locgarden's Supernatural Studies, James took a short course in vampiric law. He had a sharp mind and higher education came easily to him.

The course justified his year-long presence in Locgarden. He wasn't required to stay for the duration; he could pop back to Earth and spend time with Eliza in between his studies, yet he needed to be away from her. The look in those sharp green eyes of hers would drive him mad with guilt, imagining what she would think if she knew anything of his world.

*****

One night after university, James came back to his house with his books in hand. It was a hot night.

Neava was waiting for him. Her long blue hair was wavy and thick. She was wearing a white shirt and lacy underwear underneath. Feelings of lust engulfed James.

As he took her into his arms, she sighed heavily.

'Will you miss me when you go back to that world?' she asked, her voice full of longing.

'Yes,' James lied, for he only thought of her in the moments they were together. She was his plaything. His sex object.

'I often think how I see you almost every day, yet sometimes you smell so different or look as though so much has happened since we last spoke. I try not to think about the world beyond.'

'Don't worry on these things. You're protected from that world,' James moaned, as he longed to delve deep into her.

As they made love, James thought of nothing but how beautiful Neava was. He didn't think of Eliza, with her clever looks and smart eyes.

*****

A year passed like this. Drinking in the Kitchen, where Brandy would sit by and wait for him to return. She would look up at him with an amused expression in her eyes.

He learnt a lot on his course. All the other students were vampires; no other supernatural being dared enrol on this course, knowing the reputation the class had. A lot of the students were like James. They were killers and they revelled in the darkness of the hunger that could completely change the nature of a vampire.

Immortality was an everlasting road potentially. When one walked on the dark side, there was little chance of changing one's ways and returning to the light.

James didn't want to make friends on his course. The other students didn't try to, feeling his aura and knowing that he needed a kind of solitude.

When graduation came and he received his short course diploma in vampiric law, he chose not to attend the ceremony. He put it away with his other certificates, such as his high school diploma from Locgarden.

He avoided the company of Neava on his final night in Locgarden before he returned to London. He tidied up his home and ordered that a cleaner come. He didn't want it to smell of Neava's vanilla perfume.

*****

When he entered his flat in London, Eliza was still asleep in bed. Her beauty startled him and the image of her innocence whilst asleep overwhelmed him with guilt.

The guilt came rushing to him. It wasn't for the numerous humans he had consumed in the Kitchen in Locgarden. No, it was for Eliza and how she knew nothing of the world that he belonged to.

Chapter Thirteen

Spending a morning with innocent Eliza, who knew nothing of where he had been, was both a good and bad experience. He longed for her touch and loved how close they were getting.

Yet she knew nothing of his dark side. It scared him to imagine how it could manifest in life, even though she'd be oblivious to the time that had passed between them.

Bradley and Jessica were soon to be wed. James was looking forward to the stag do with

Bradley and some of their mates. It was to be held at a very exclusive bar in London, where they had rented the upstairs to hold the party.

*****

As the days passed away from the magical realm, a sobering feeling cleansed James of the intoxication that he had been indulging in. Thoughts of the blood of innocent victims often coloured his dreams and filled him with a dark lust.

When he was with Eliza, he was aware he was more animalistic and rougher in bed. She commented on these facts, stating it was like something had gotten into him.

'It must be something in the water, I guess,' James said, after making wild, passionate love to Eliza.

'As much as it is thrilling, maybe we could keep to drinking water for once in a blue moon. I haven't the energy to keep up with you,' Eliza said. Her hair was messed up and she had sweat beads on her brow.

'I love you dearly, Eliza,' he said, kissing her gently on the lips, 'I'm sure the beast inside of me will quell. I hope I didn't frighten you with how wild I've been lately in bed?'

Eliza blushed a deep pink. 'Not frightened, it just shocked me a little, I must admit. It seems to have come from nowhere.'

James knew that to be false. The beast inside him was already desiring more of the innocent blood he had enjoyed in the magical realm. This he knew was why he was making love to Eliza with such rough passion. It was why his body felt hot all the time.

As the sky became dark, James enjoyed the closeness to Eliza as she slept. He felt a sense of agitation that shivered through his body. He very much wanted to get up and morph into an animal. He knew he was also craving the magical realm. Yet he must stay away for a while, or else he would lose himself in the blood as it danced and mingled with all his senses. He would become senseless to the intoxication of the death that he danced with.

*****

A week later, James found his senses were clearing up. He still longed for the magical realm and felt as though he had become somewhat addicted to his life there.

In dreams, he remembered the Kitchen, where he had freely taken innocent victims who had been bred for his enjoyment by capitalist vampires. These vampires cared nothing for the humans who were doomed by the magic that hid them from the rest of Locgarden.

James often thought of his time studying vampiric law and what it had taught him about his legacy as a vampire. A lot of the law that he learnt about in the short course was old law that had long been changed by more progressive thinkers. He learnt about the history of his kind and it was very clear how they felt a sense of entitlement to the things they enjoyed because of their immortality.

He knew his mother had been a blood drinker. It had been what got her killed by a vampire hunter. He didn't often like to think about his mother. She was a memory he stuffed away and very scarcely lamented on.

*****

James accompanied Bradley and a few friends to Club Eighty-Four. Tonight was Bradley's stag do. He was to be married next week to Jessica.

The small group had booked the whole club for the night. The blue décor and fairy lights that lit up beautiful works of art made the club classy, with an exclusive air.

Bradley had only invited two friends apart from James to his celebration. James guessed Bradley had surrendered to the habits of married life already.

One of Bradley's friends was a work colleague and the other an old university friend. Bradley was wearing a light blue suit and looked classy.

'This will be one of your last nights of freedom. You sure about your decision not to have any strippers?' James asked, as he nudged Bradley.

'Oh, don't be silly,' Bradley said with a blush, 'I wouldn't dream of doing such a thing.'

As James took one of the champagne glasses offered to him by an attractive male waiter in his early twenties, his mind wandered far away from this realm. What would Bradley think of him if he knew that all the time that they had known each other, since primary school, he had lived another existence that Bradley wouldn't even be able to comprehend?

James felt sad as he sipped the champagne. He loved his life here, yet he knew that the foundation of his character was built on his second life in the magical realm. His easy-going confidence resided in the fact that he knew that he was an immortal being. He did not fear death or anything in this world.

Bradley's friends talked amongst themselves and made little effort with James. It amused James because he saw similarities in them to Bradley – that awkward shyness that some people possess.

At last, Bradley's friend from university came up to James. He was a dorkish-looking young man with a large mole on his face and was dressed far too much like he was going on an archaeology outing.

'Hi, I'm Vincent,' he said.

'So, you know James from university?'

'Yes, he was studying Economics with me. I know, not the most exciting subject. I always wished I'd studied Archaeology,' Vincent said with a smile.

'Well, there's always books and magazines to indulge in.'

'Yeah, indeed. Well, if I ever win the lottery, I'm going back to university to become an archaeologist. Not like we can all see £9,000 a year in fees as pocket money … no offence.'

'None taken,' said James with a smile. 'Come on, Vincent, let's get some more drinks. This bachelor party is feeling more like an old ladies tea party.'

James accompanied Vincent to the drinks bar. Soon, all four men were downing shots and laughing about memories they had. Bradley's three friends recalled incidents that were comical.

'Do you remember that boy … oh, what was his name? Anyway, we had a presentation for an essay on economic trends and he only goes and performs a Britney Spears song and dance routine. That guy was funny,' Vincent said.

'The professor for that class was too nice; she let him add that to his presentation,' Bradley said with a laugh.

The men drank a lot and when the club closed at two in the morning, they were all hammered. They got an Uber back to the hotel, where Bradley had paid for them to all stay for the night.

It was a smart hotel but not overly posh. The men had a few more drinks, but soon everyone except James was ready for bed.

'I think we better retire to our rooms for a bit of sleep,' Bradley said.

'Oh come on, man! It's your freaking stag do!' James shouted in a drunken manner.

'Goodnight, James,' Bradley said, as he hugged his friend.

'Fine! Goodnight,' said James with a laugh.

James made his way to his hotel room. It was comfortable and clean. He switched on the flat screen TV, wondering whether he should watch a movie.

'Not good enough,' James said with a sigh. He knew where his body ached to go. He knew where he must return to.

Chapter Fourteen

In the privacy of his hotel, James entered the magical realm. Here he was happy. He knew where he wanted to go and how he would feed deep on human life.

As he looked around his house in the realm, he smiled to himself, thinking how clean and lovely the décor was. Yet then he noticed that Neava was waiting for him.

His thoughts turned to a different kind of hunger, a deep lust that brewed inside him for his beautiful blue-haired possession. He owned Neava by her own choosing, yet no man had ever enjoyed her soft and delicious flesh.

'Neava,' he cooed.

'I must speak with you about something very important,' she said.

'Yeah, yeah. Later,' he said, moving his hands over her brown dress in preparation to undress her.

She slapped his hand away. 'No, James. I must speak with you seriously at once.'

James sobered himself up, willing his power to produce the effect that would leave him feeling as clear as day.

'I'm sober now. Completely blooming sober. So, what was it you wanted to tell me?' asked James with a chuckle.

'You must be aware that I have new protection over me. A witch that you don't know and will not find. So, if you try and harm me, her magic will open the spell and it will be just …' Neava's voice was full of fear.

'What on Earth are you on about? I'm all the protection you could ever need.'

'I know that you love a girl outside the realm,' Neava trembled.

'It doesn't mean I don't care for you, Neava. We've always had this realm to enjoy together.'

'Yes, I know. But I want more. I want to be what you are, a vampire. Now, if you say no, do not think that there will not be any consequences. For I will end my own life and the magic bound to my life will send visions into your realm. Visions that will make Eliza see what you really are.'

James's mind was racing with furious thoughts. He had never wanted to hurt Neava. Even in this awful moment, he did not desire to kill her. Yet he did want to hit her hard.

He knew he was backed into a corner. He was terrified because he recognised a needy side in Neava, which had drawn her to him. A woman of her beauty could have married a rich man in the realm and had children who were doted on. Yet

Neava had chosen to be a sex slave to him, a vampire, whose only real offer in return was protection until the day she died a natural death.

'You're not lying to me about the witch, are you?'

'Let me show you the amulet that bounds magic to me and potentially Eliza, should any harm come to me,' Neava said, revealing a golden amulet.

James could feel the magic buzzing off the object; he knew that its magic was dangerous. His drunken state earlier had been why he hadn't bothered to notice the item, yet there were many magical items in his home.

'What choice do I have?'

'The choice is yours. Either I die at your or my own hands and Eliza learns the truth, or you turn me into a vampire and I will be satisfied.'

James took a deep breath as curiosity and hunger quelled inside of him. He had never taken much of her blood. How strange it would feel to deeply feed on her.

'I will do it,' said James with a sigh. He moved Neava's long hair away from her neck, revealing her soft tanned skin. As he drew his fangs to the surface and delved deep into her neck, she sighed heavily.

He drank softly yet deeply, taking the strength out of her body quickly. He held her around the waist, supporting her body as her legs lost their strength.

He saw images in her blood of secrets he had always known. How she had loved him from the moment they had met. How her heart had been filled with curiosity and wonder by him. A man half-morph and half-vampire. Immortal yet also a shapeshifter.

Her blood tasted beautiful – of the fresh fruits and spices that she ate. Her clean diet made her blood taste divine. Her soul was needy and longing, and it was intoxicating to search that soul as he drank from her.

As her heart began to slow, James forced himself to withdraw from taking her life. He looked at her for a flicker of a moment as she was close to death.

As he bit his own wrist deeply and forced the wound to her mouth, she could do nothing but drink the vampiric blood. As she drank, her heartbeat grew stronger again with every moment.

A fierce spirit entered her as she became immortal. As the spirit of the vampire entered her body, she flung James across the living room.

As James quickly got up and watched the spectacle, he was somewhat curious to see a human be made immortal by his own hands. He had never turned anyone before tonight.

Neava moaned and groaned as she turned. Her body convulsed and shook. She was foaming at the mouth and uttering words in ancient vampiric languages she didn't understand.

As James picked her up and carried her to his bed, he wondered what she would be like now that she was immortal. He feared she would be angry to know that James was no longer sexually interested in her as his plaything.

As the newly turning vampire slept, James dimmed the lights and fetched some of his old sketch books. Neava and James had enjoyed a playful relationship. Sometimes, James had enjoyed painting her naked, knowing no one but he would ever see the provocative images.

As he looked through his sketches, he found a picture that made his heart feel sad. An image of Neava looking innocent and beautiful with a sheet over her naked body.

Eliza had no idea that James could draw so well. Yet James was a vampire and this meant he was pretty much good at all artistic talents.

'Sleep well, my lover,' James whispered softly.

Neava was speaking in an ancient vampiric language still, her words soft and uneasy. He thought he heard the word which meant 'spirit', yet the words were so old.

As she slept and became immersed in a new life as an immortal, James felt a new connection with her. He had turned her and now they would always be connected in this way.

Neava didn't wake until the following night. She looked paler, yet it was only because she had not fed. The misconception that vampires were the undead was simply false. They were a product of something else, belonging to the magical realm. Yet they were not the undead.

James watched as Neava tried her best to compose herself, to look sexy and alluring to him after everything that had happened. She was still one of the most beautiful women that James had ever met.

'I can feel we've changed,' she eventually whispered.

'Things will never be the same between us.'

'Will you find another plaything to enjoy like you did with me?' Neava asked simply.

'I don't know. I suppose eventually I will get lonely. When I'm not with Eliza. There will never be another Neava. Yet I suppose I will want someone young and beautiful in this realm.'

'Maybe next time, you shouldn't pick someone as smart as me,' Neava said, laughing bitterly. 'I suspect that might be a good idea,' she said. 'I need to feed now. I feel the longing for blood so strongly.'

'You will learn to control that. I have books on living as a newly turned vampire that I can give you. I can guide you through this whole process …'

'No. Just give me one thing. James, I want you to be there when I feed for the first time. I'll need those books as well.'

'As if I wouldn't help you learn to adjust. Honestly, Neava!'

She was quiet and looked sadly up at him with tears in her eyes. 'We are no longer lovers. I can feel how the sexual chemistry has expired for you in the act of changing me. I am no longer what you desire in a mistress. So, I ask this, that you take me to feed just once. Then I will leave.'

*****

James waited for Neava to bathe and change her clothes. She looked beautiful in a blue flowing dress that he recalled her having worn often before. Yet he didn't long for her slender curves the way he always had before tonight.

He looked upon her with new, uninterested eyes. He would be glad when she had finished feeding and was done with this place.

He gave her the money that her home in Locgarden had cost and she signed over the deeds back to him. He didn't know what to do with the little cosy house.

As they walked in silence to the witches' quarter to seek out Brandy, James felt a cold sense of bitterness. He was bitter that his mistress was now a sexless creature to him.

He knew that it was the dynamics of their relationship which had made him feel this way upon turning her. No man could ever truly own her again. They would have the whole of eternity to avoid each other.

James let Neava feed alone in the Kitchen club. The waitress tried to make conversation with him about how he had turned a mortal. Yet he snapped away all of her questions.

When it was done, Neava was left buzzing from the blood. So full of that blood that her thoughts were beyond lamenting on James.

'If I ever need you, I will call upon you. I even have your number still, so if you ignore my call, I can annoy you by text.'

'This is goodbye. Farewell, Neava,' James said.

He watched her board a train, leaving Locgarden. Which stop and where she was going, he didn't know. He didn't want to know. She had enough money to live comfortably anywhere in the realm. She would find witches to guide her to places like the Kitchen. Or she may even choose to live somewhere where vampires held more power.

Wherever she went, she was out of his life. Neava was now just a memory of a girl he had greatly longed for and owned for over a decade. He had never loved her the way he did with Eliza. Yet his enjoyment of owning her had created in him an affection for her that ran deep. It was painful to experience that caring turn to cold resentment.

Chapter Fifteen

James loved Eliza. He knew that. He adored every inch of her body and cherished what they had together. Yet now everything had changed because she was pregnant.

Eliza didn't know yet. She didn't take the pill, stating how a cousin of hers had gained a lot of weight from it. Eliza and James had been careful not to conceive a baby.

Yet James knew that a new life was brewing inside of her. It wasn't past the point of abortion, yet it was a magical baby and wouldn't leave her body easily like a mortal child.

James could feel the baby brewing inside of Eliza. He could feel the seed of magic growing within the foetus. He knew the child would be part-morph and part-vampire. Yet unlike James, it would be part-mortal.

He knew that Agnes would know about the child soon; perhaps the child already had a guide who was being called from the magical realm.

It was too early to say, yet James wondered if Eliza had felt the change. Soon the magic would open her eyes to a new reality beyond this world.

'I bet my sister looks great in the dress she's chosen,' Eliza said, as she dressed. 'Mum was really picky about what dress she picked, you know her.'

'So, she picked Jessica's dress?' James asked with a laugh.

'Yes, she did,' Eliza said, combing her hair as she looked in the mirror. 'Of course, Jessica didn't mind.'

'Moreen is quite a character.'

'Yes, Mother has always dreamed of Jessica's wedding day. She's her golden girl.'

As Eliza prepared herself for the wedding, James daydreamed just a little. She would be bound to him now, forever, because of the child growing inside of her.

James knew how a morph or indeed vampire child was conceived; unlike a normal baby, the supernatural being had to want the child to exist on a deep level of their core. James knew this and he believed that his inner desires must be right.

As the couple travelled to the church where Bradley and Jessica were to be wed, they were in a happy place. James played peaceful classical music on the car journey.

At the pretty little church, which was located in Mayfair, they saw how Moreen was waiting outside for them. She smiled and waved energetically.

Moreen lightly hugged her daughter and smiled warmly at James. She was dressed in a pastel blue dress and a hat with a flower. She really was the spitting image of a much older Jessica. Her facial features were lined from years of smoking, yet it was evident that she was still a beautiful woman even with all the markings of age.

'You look beautiful, Eliza,' Moreen said.

'Thank you, Mother,' Eliza replied, blushing ever so slightly.

James could feel that Eliza was taken aback by the compliment from her mother, which illustrated a lot about their relationship. James could also feel the truths inside of Moreen's heart. That indeed Jessica was her favourite child. Although Moreen loved Eliza, she found it hard to relate to her.

'Your dad's already in the church, let's get inside,' Moreen said.

James and Eliza followed Moreen into the church. The building was beautiful and had a calm air to it. They took their seats next to Eliza's parents.

Neither the bride nor groom had invited a lot of people. The church was only half-full. The music commenced, with a pianist playing the wedding song.

Jessica looked delicate and beautiful in her dress. James imagined how wonderful it would be to experience a wedding with Eliza as his own bride.

James felt the nerves exuding off Bradley. He was anxious being in front of all these people. His friend was besotted with Jessica. They truly were soulmates.

As the vicar asked the couple to recite their vows, Moreen began to cry.

'Do you, Bradley Mitchell, take thee, Jessica Barnet, to be your lawful wedded wife? To love and to cherish from this day forward?' asked the vicar.

'I do,' replied Bradley.

The vicar asked the same question to Jessica, who smiled warmly upon Bradley.

'I do take Bradley to be my husband,' Jessica said.

As the couple were announced husband and wife, James felt the collective happiness of the two of them. James didn't often like to use his morph powers upon people, yet he saw things in their future which weren't as bright as they were currently expecting. He saw divorce in their paths just two years down the line.

James used his morph powers to alter this direction and make them bound together in love and happiness until the fatal day where Bradley would die of a heart attack aged seventy-seven.

Bradley would be a happier man for the direction of his destiny, which James had now changed. James felt that it was a good gift to give his best mortal friend.

As the couple left the church and took cars towards the wedding party, everyone was in a happy mood and oblivious to the magical changes in destiny which had taken place through James.

The wedding party was quiet, which well matched the newly-wed couple's true personalities. Moreen drank a little too much champagne.

Her husband Howard Barnet was quiet. He looked smart in his suit. He congratulated his daughter and new son-in-law on their wedding. He seemed very impressed by the food at the party reception.

'Oh, Howard,' scoffed Moreen, as she watched her husband get his third plate of fancy hors d'oeuvres.

'It's a special occasion. No one seems to be enjoying the food. I might as well,' Howard said, as he continued to fill his plate.

'Eliza!' exclaimed her mother, catching the eye of her daughter.

Eliza smiled as she walked over to her mother, with James at her side. 'The wedding ceremony was lovely, wasn't it.'

'Yes, darling, it was. Isn't it exciting that they'll be swanning off to LA.'

'Yes, Mother. The art scene in Los Angeles is meant to be amazing. I recommended a few places for Jessica to visit.'

'Oh, you would recommend something arty,' Moreen said, huffing.

'James and I are going to get some drinks.'

'Fine,' Moreen said, as she made her way to greet Jessica once more.

Jessica and Bradley were having the time of their lives. James enjoyed the collective happiness in the party reception.

When the party ended that night at midnight, everyone said their farewells to the newly wedded couple, who were off for a month in LA at a five-star hotel.

'Look after Bradley,' James said, as he hugged Jessica.

'Oh, well, of course. Take care of my sis,' she said, beaming.

'Have a wonderful honeymoon,' James said.

James watched Jessica get into the limo with Bradley. They were off to a fancy hotel before jetting off to America the following afternoon.

Chapter Sixteen

Eliza was very content with life. She had a few weeks left of her Master's degree before she would know how she had done on the course. From the feedback she had received, she was on track to get a distinction in her Master of Fine Arts.

As she worked on a piece for her private collection of art, which wasn't part of her coursework, she listened to indie music on Spotify. The sound of a soft and melodic male voice filled the room beautifully.

The painting would be kept secret. It was a portrait of James. She had drawn his image in pencil and was now filling the canvas with bold abstract colours.

She thought to herself, as she worked on the large canvas, about how life was going so well. Soon, she would be receiving her Master's degree and booking the graduation.

Jessica would be back from Los Angeles by then and she could arrange the details of attending the graduation ceremony with her sister. She had already picked a nice dress from Zara which she planned to wear for the ceremony. It would be in November, so she would wear her favourite grey coat, which was slimming yet understated.

She already had plans to pursue a PhD in September. She was besotted with studying art. She knew her mum wouldn't be impressed with the idea of her studying for three more years and not working. Yet she was soon to be moving in with James.

She was nervous about the prospect but also excited for the change. She already stayed at his flat half the week as it was these days. She kept art materials in his spare bedroom.

James had recently asked her to move in. It was a big step for the couple, yet she loved him with all her heart.

*****

James was to meet with Maggie in the magical realm. As he waited for her to arrive at a quaint little café, he enjoyed the cool air of summer. He drank strong coffee as the warm weather gently caressed his skin.

Maggie arrived at the café shortly after; she was wearing a black dress and chunky heels. Her long blonde hair was pin straight. She smiled as she took a seat opposite James in the café.

'So, what was this news you had to tell me?' Maggie asked.

'Well, it's a big one.'

'What?' Maggie asked, picking up her menu.

'Eliza's pregnant,' James said.

Maggie bit her lip and raised a questioning eyebrow. 'A magical baby … has she begun to form a key yet?'

'No, the baby is too new to change her life just yet. But in a month or so, she will know that I am magical. She won't know I'm a vampire, because I am not planning on telling her. I just can't, all the questions she'll have …'

'You don't want her to know about your dark side,' Maggie replied.

'Exactly. What would sweet Eliza think? Someone so gentle and nearly completely pure; if she knew that I got a kick out of killing innocent people in this realm …' James whispered.

'When are you going to tell her? Does she know she's pregnant?'

'No …' James said. 'She has no idea.'

The mortal waiter arrived to take Maggie's order. Maggie coldly addressed the female waitress, asking for a glass of red wine. When the waitress left, she continued to discuss matters with James.

'Why don't we go hunting tonight?'

'You mean visit the Kitchen?' James asked with a sigh.

'No … I mean hunt here in Locgarden. You're going to have Eliza be able to enter this realm soon. She'll be sleeping in your bed and a magical resident by the blood right of her child. Surely you want to have some fun before your freedom here is capped.'

'I don't know. I thought you'd be giving me advice about the responsibilities of fatherhood.'

'My advice is that you have fun while you can,' Maggie said with a smirk.

'I could be persuaded,' James said with a sigh. 'If you promise not to tell anyone, ever.'

'Have I ever said a word about what we do? No one knows about our hunting expeditions or the visits to the Kitchen. Only Brandy holds that secret.'

'You've twisted my arm enough. Let's go hunting,' James said, smiling as thoughts of the thrill of the hunt rushed into his mind.

They soon left the quiet café. James followed Maggie into the deep depths of the city of Locgarden. They had both had enough of talking; now was the time to take action on what they both deeply desired. The hunt – it was the greatest of intoxications for the two vampires.

Maggie led the way, looking sleek and like a panther on the prowl. She moved with precision as she scanned the quiet streets. Locgarden was a huge city and the pair stalked the city for a while, simply enjoying the scenes of potential victims.

Yet as night fell into deep darkness, it was time. Maggie stopped and looked at James with such excitement in her eyes. She motioned to a girl who was hidden behind the safety of a home. The girl was home alone and sleeping soundly in her bedroom. She was aged seventeen and completely innocent.

The two vampires easily cracked the window open. The girl with long brown hair and fair skin didn't rouse from her slumber.

Maggie prodded the girl and used her powers upon the teenager.

'Who are you?' the girl asked in a dreamy voice.

'I am death. It's time to embrace me,' Maggie whispered.

The girl was under a vampiric compulsion induced by Maggie and James. She couldn't fight back.

'I don't wish to die. Please, take someone else,' the girl whispered.

'No, you must die. Give me your arm and the other to my friend,' Maggie said.

The girl obeyed. Maggie and James both took an arm and delved into her wrists with their fangs. They drank slowly, knowing that the girl would be alone till tomorrow. They took their time enjoying the compulsion and how it made the girl's thoughts slow. Yet the compulsion couldn't wash away the sadness that the girl experienced.

She fell into death easily as the two vampires drank from her. When she was dead, Maggie tucked her back into bed, throwing the cover over her. Maggie laughed to herself as the two vampires left the scene of murder.

'Such fun,' Maggie said.

'It's quite an intoxication,' James replied, breathing heavily.

'Your Eliza will be entering this realm soon. My poor James will have to hide his true nature … for a time, anyway.'

'Eliza will never know of my darkness, for as long as her life with me is something pure that has brought a child into the world. I can't do these things again for as long as Eliza lives with me.'

'When she dies of old age, your grief will be great. Then we can feed here. Maybe your child will join us; we can show him or her their birthright.'

'Maybe. Maybe. Let us leave this place,' James said.

Maggie and James left the scene and soon made their way back to James's home. There they drank strong black coffee, which was always the most pleasant thing to drink after the blood of innocent victims.

'I might not call you for a while, once Eliza is introduced to this realm. But you do understand that I will miss your company?' James asked.

'I know. She will be mortal and you do not want her to know all the truths of your identity. I understand and respect your decision.'

Maggie and James spent time reminiscing on things before the sun came up. When it was dawn, Maggie bid James farewell and vowed that she would see him soon but not too soon.

James slept in his bed and experienced uneasy dreams. Thoughts of a dark shadow and the sound of a female scream consumed his nightmares.

James spent the next few days reading about supernatural pregnancies. He wondered what his child's guide would be like. He wondered when the magical key upon a necklace would start to appear on Eliza. He knew he must ease her into the revelation. He knew that, if needed, he could change her mind regarding how she reacted with his morph powers. Yet he wanted to give Eliza free will in all things regarding how she reacted to the revelation.

Chapter Seventeen

James was ready to tell Eliza the truth. The baby had been brewing inside of her for a month. Some women might have noticed a child growing within them, yet Eliza had not experienced morning sickness.

As Eliza bathed in the bathroom, James could see her naked form because of his morph powers. He gazed upon the gentle beauty of her elegant body through a vision in his mind.

He knew it was time as she soaked in the bath, the berry-scented shower gel filling the air with its sweet intoxication. As he listened in on her aura, he knew she was extremely happy. So happy that she hardly believed that things were going so well. He knew that Eliza had never expected to find love in her life.

When Eliza got out of the bath, she wrapped a white towel around her slender form. She made her way into their bedroom, for she had now moved into his flat.

'Eliza,' James said.

'You'll be late for work if you don't get a move on,' Eliza said, her voice soft and worry-free.

'I've called in sick.'

'You OK? You don't look sick. What's wrong?'

'I need to tell you something,' James said, fretting on how to show her.

'What's wrong?'

James knew that Eliza would be frightened by the revelation. He knew it could induce a great deal of terror in mortals to know of a world beyond their scope of things. James induced a great calm in her, along with a sense of acceptance that would alter her state of feelings and how she reacted to his news.

'Eliza, how are you feeling?'

Eliza smiled dreamily at James. 'Oh, it's strange, I feel so calm all of a sudden, as if I'm stoned, yet I've never smoked weed in my life. But I imagine this is how it must feel.'

'Well, that's that. Listen, you're going to be shocked with the news that I'm about to tell you. Yet because I have induced you with a calming sensation, you will accept the news and love me regardless of any upset feelings you have. Any sadness you feel about your ordinary world shattering will melt away like ice on a summer's day.'

'Of course it will. Now, tell me, what is this news?' Eliza asked, smiling.

James didn't need to tell her. He showed her. He touched her stomach and it glowed as though a brilliant light had illuminated it from inside.

'My … my stomach. Is there some sort of glow-worm inside of me?' Eliza asked, chuckling under the influence of James's magic.

'No, Eliza. You are pregnant with my child and it will be a magical being of morph descent,' James said, not mentioning that the child would also be half-vampire.

Eliza's eyes lit up and she began to cry. They were tears of joy because her heart was truly happy with the news. She wanted this child at the core of her being. It made James truly ecstatic to see this revelation in her.

'I love you, Eliza. In time, this child will become more conscious. In a few months, you'll be able to see that you are wearing a necklace with a key upon it. How your particular necklace will look I do not yet know. Yet that necklace will allow you to enter a magical reality where my people come from.'

'So, you're a magical creature?' Eliza asked.

'Yes, Eliza. Because you are carrying a magical child, you'll have access to the magical realm for all the days of your life.'

'Tell me everything about this world that you've kept secret from me,' Eliza said.

James began to describe the magical realm in as much detail as he could. He used his power to draw images, which were like holographic scenes of memories he could recall from life in the realm.

Eliza remarked on how Locgarden looked like nothing she had ever seen. She was in awe of the images that he invoked all around them.

James described how he had always led a double life, entering the great city of Locgarden and attending school there for the supernatural. He described how at the same time he had always lived the life that Eliza knew of. How he had indeed met Bradley in the middle school he attended in this world.

By the end of the afternoon, Eliza was aware more of James's truth than she ever had been before. She didn't know of his dark, secret adventures killing innocent people. James intended that she would never know of this. Through his magical influence, he could keep this a secret from her forever.

In some ways, he knew it was wrong because she would be oblivious to the fact that her own child was part-vampire. Yet James believed it was the only way he could live with himself, knowing that he was a killer and being aware this would break her heart.

As the afternoon drew to 3 p.m., the couple ate lunch. Eliza was emotionally exhausted from the effects of the magic and the revelation that she was having a morph baby.

She soon fell asleep after the meal of sandwiches washed down with some decaf tea. When she slept uneasily in the bed, murmuring to herself as her subconscious did its best to deal with the new truths, James made use of her sleeping to connect with the baby.

When James had touched Eliza's stomach with his magic, the child had awoken to its magical senses. He listened to the aura of the child growing inside of Eliza. It's morph and vampire qualities were in equal measure.

'Child of mine,' he whispered, only audible enough that the unborn baby would hear him, 'promise me that you'll keep your vampiric identity a secret from your mother.'

The child did not reply, yet James felt its soul brewing inside of Eliza. He felt how the new foetus already loved its mother.

*****

The days passed gently by. Eliza was in an easy state of mind, which she was quite aware was being induced by James. She was unable to quarrel, whether she was OK about this in her mind or not.

She hadn't told any of her friends or family that she was pregnant yet. She had noticed the outline of a fine chain upon her neck. Yet there was no sign of a key just yet.

James had informed her that the key would show itself in time, when her child's magical guide was ready. Whoever they were, they had already been called upon.

Eliza had spent the last few days doodling images of Locgarden from the visions James had invoked. She imagined how strange it would feel when she finally entered the city and made herself at home in the property James owned there.

James had informed her how there were as many cities in 'the realm', as the people of his world called it, as there were on Earth. Locgarden belonged to a country called Lazcape. The city of Locgarden had a population of 500,000, of which around 10,000 were supernatural.

Eliza was glad that she had fallen in love with James. She knew that she was happier knowing about this realm than if she had lived her whole life in ignorance of it. She wasn't sure if James would have ever told her about it if she had not been pregnant with his magical child.

The idea of this realm frightened her as well as excited her. James had gone back to work today. She was alone in the house, yet she was now aware how his magic protected her from afar. How if he chose, he could view her from wherever she was.

Eliza had recently received her results for her Master's degree. She had received a distinction for her studies from Chelsea College of Arts.

Jessica and James had shown more enthusiasm than her mother. At the time, Eliza had expressed how she wanted to study a PhD. Yet now the idea seemed overwhelming.

As Eliza got up from the sofa in James's flat where she now lived, she realised that her tea was cold.

'I bet my baby could warm that tea,' Eliza said, laughing to herself as she imagined her future child.

Eliza went into the bedroom that she shared with James. She fired up her laptop and began to write a list. She would no longer pursue a PhD just yet. She would work somewhere sensible like Jessica did. She would bring up her child to love art. One day, when it was older, she would go back to school. Yet she believed her job now was to educate this magical child that was brewing inside of her.

Chapter Eighteen

It was the day of Eliza's Master's graduation. She was wearing a loosely fitting floral dress that didn't overemphasize her baby bump.

Eliza felt proud of herself for all she had achieved in her academic life. She was a great artist, and even though she was modest, she knew that she was talented.

Her whole world had changed recently. She was no longer simply the art student who lived with her parents in Chesham. She was a woman who was having a magical pregnancy, to a man who could shapeshift and stop time.

'You look smart,' Moreen said, as she handed over a cup of decaf tea to Eliza.

'Thank you, Mother,' Eliza replied.

'So, you're really going to put your plans on hold for future study? I do think you're making the right decision,' Moreen said.

'Yes, Mother, I am,' Eliza said.

Moreen was over the moon about the baby. Since Eliza had announced that she was having James's baby, Moreen had treated her differently. Eliza felt it was because Moreen valued married women and mothers with more respect than she did single women. It was part of Moreen's simplistic attitude that women should be kept in some respect. That they should belong to someone.

Moreen left Eliza alone with her tea to continue getting ready for the big day. The graduation ceremony was at the O2 in London. Jessica was to attend with her.

As Eliza waited in her room for Jessica to finish getting ready, she thought about how her secret new life changed her relationship with her family. She would soon be visiting a dimension unknown to them. They would never know of the secret world that belonged to Eliza and her baby.

Eliza looked in the mirror of her dresser; she was now clearly showing. Her parents were soon to be packing up her stuff so that she could move in to James's spacious flat. They had hired a removal van.

It was weird to think that her room would be empty soon. She had lived in this house all her life. All the collective energy in the room amazed her as she thought back to all the memories.

Jessica knocked on her door. 'It's me,' she said.

'Come in, Jessica.'

Married life was treating Jessica well. She was still working in the local Superdrug as she wanted her own independence from Bradley's wealth.

Both Bradley and James were from millionaire families. Bradley owned a beautiful house in Battersea, yet he was soon to be renting it out so that he could move to Chesham. Jessica and Bradley had got a joint mortgage on a property.

'You look beautiful,' Jessica said to Eliza. Jessica was looking radiant, with her long blonde hair tied in a high ponytail and her slender figure clinging to a modest black dress.

'It's weird to think Mum and Dad won't have us here anymore. Strange to think of our bedrooms empty in a few weeks,' Eliza said.

'I'm excited to move into the new house. But yes, I'll miss seeing Mum and Dad all the time,' Jessica said.

Jessica and Bradley had bought a new build Barratt property close to the end of town. It had cost half a million pounds and Bradley's trust fund secured the mortgage more than Jessica's earnings.

'I am excited at the thought of visiting you there,' Eliza said.

'Maybe in a year or so, I'll be expecting a little one with Bradley. We've discussed it, you know; we both want children.'

'He's such a nice man,' Eliza said. 'You would both make wonderful parents.'

Eliza and Jessica said goodbye to Moreen as they set off for Eliza's graduation. Their father Howard was at work. He worked in a garden centre in Wendover, which was a nearby town. He worked even though the mortgage had been paid off ten years earlier.

Moreen and Howard had been lucky to get the right to buy on their council property. They had worked hard and always done their best for their daughters. Neither Moreen nor Howard had degrees, yet they were both intelligent in different ways.

Howard was a very quiet man but had a calm wisdom about him. He was a gentle and kind person who had always brought his daughters up with a great deal of understanding.

Moreen was very much someone who could remember everything that was going on in her favourite soaps. She remembered all the details of what her family members were doing and who was married to whom. She had that sort of mind.

Eliza and Jessica travelled on the train to the O2 in Greenwich. They took the Metropolitan train part of the way and then got the Jubilee line.

The O2 was a modern building that had originally been the Millennium Dome. Eliza handed the security guard their tickets and they found their seats for the graduation ceremony.

Eliza was seated with other students from her class, while Jessica sat with the friends and family of graduates in a different area of the audience.

Eliza had made a few friends on her course, who she occasionally went to the cinema with or to a quiet pub. She was seated next to people on the course who she hadn't particularly clicked with, yet she could see her friends Helen and Daphne were seated nearby.

The music that introduced the honorary graduates was cheesy. It was played by a quartet of trumpets that created a musical sense of prestige for the event.

Eliza was nervous when she took her plaque, which symbolised her degree. Eliza watched the other graduates take their prizes and enjoyed the formality of the event.

She remembered how three years ago she had been doing this for her bachelor's degree. Her world was unrecognisable now compared to what it had been then. Eliza knew that she wanted her art to embody some of the change that she had been experiencing.

After the graduation ceremony, Jessica and Eliza went for a celebratory meal at Wagamama. There were a lot of restaurants and a large cinema in the O2. It was a huge building.

They enjoyed their time together. They talked about their plans and how excited they both were about Eliza's baby. Eliza was sad that she knew Jessica would never know about the magic.

Eliza had seen James shapeshift into a wolf. Jessica would never know of any of these magical powers. Her life with Bradley was very different to Eliza's life with James.

When the sisters got back to their family home in Chesham, Moreen asked to see the graduation photos.

'You're glowing,' Moreen said. 'I'm proud of you for sticking at your studies. I know I'm not the best mum, but I am proud that you stuck to your dreams.'

Eliza felt hot tears in her eyes, 'Mum, I know you are. Here, let's watch some TV together.'

Moreen's face lit up. 'Oh yes, let's. We hardly ever watch TV together.'

'I'll make the tea,' Howard said, as he lifted Chloe the cat off his lap and walked into the kitchen.

The four of them watched TV together. Moreen picked *EastEnders* to watch, as she never liked to miss an episode. After *EastEnders*, they watched *Love Island*, which was another one of Moreen's guilty pleasures. Eliza commented on how *Love Island* was 'the most ridiculous programme she had ever seen'!

Chapter Nineteen

Eliza felt as though the past few months had gone by in a haze. She felt as if James may have been influencing her mood ever since his revelation when she was one month into her pregnancy.

She was now eight months gone and excited about the upcoming birth of her baby boy. The key had finally shown on her necklace, which only magical beings could see.

Not only could she see the key and felt ready to soon enter the magical realm, but she could also now see the keys of so-called normal people in this world who had obviously been living double lives in the magical realm. A woman in her local Tesco surprised her, when Eliza noticed she was wearing one of the magical necklaces.

James's father Earl had been very supportive of the pregnancy. He seemed excited at the prospect of becoming a grandfather. As Eliza and James visited his property in Mayfair, Eliza was preparing to enter the magical realm for the first time.

'I was born there, and it isn't so strange,' Earl said. 'I know this is a life-changing secret you have, one a mortal wouldn't even remember if you told them; see, you're not mortal anymore. You're a magical woman by the lineage of your morph son.'

'I can't wait to meet him,' Eliza said.

'Oh, I can already see things about that son of yours. He's going to be a better man than his father,' Earl said, smiling sadly.

'Oh, well … I look forward to seeing this realm,' Eliza said, not really understanding what Earl meant by his comment.

Earl drew the heavy red curtains and Eliza watched as he got his key out of its chain. Earl's chain was thick and had an antique look to it.

'I haven't used this key since your mother's funeral,' Earl said to his son.

'I know, Dad. Times are moving on. It's finally time to go back to Locgarden and the realm,' James said.

'We shall go to your childhood house,' Earl said, as he opened the doorway to the magical realm.

James held Eliza's hand as the circular door was visible to the three of them. He held her hand tight as she gasped.

'Come on, my love, don't be scared,' James said, as they entered the magical realm.

As Eliza stepped through for the first time into the magical realm, she felt a sense of adrenalin. She had entered a magical dimension beyond the scope of her family and friends.

Looking around her, she could see that she was standing outside of James's family home. It was a grand building with purple paint decorating the high and prestigious house. There was ivory growing on the sides of the building. It looked well maintained.

'Oh, what memories I have of this house,' Earl said. 'Come on in,' he said, motioning to Eliza and James as he opened the door to his family home in Locgarden.

The living room was spacious. There was a painting on the wall of James as a baby. Eliza could see the image of Earl as a younger man and his late wife Stephanie in the painting.

'The property has been maintained all these years that have passed since I last visited. Time has moved as I wished, for the key knows when you wish for time to move on in the magical realm with one's absence,' Earl said, more to himself than to Eliza or James.

Eliza felt excited to be in the realm; she wanted to explore, yet was also frightened by this prospect.

'Eliza, let me show you some of our memories. Come on, boy, you won't be able to show her soon enough,' Earl said, motioning to his son to follow him into the basement of the house.

Inside the huge basement, there were boxes of history from the morph generations that had come before Earl.

'I keep precious memories. I remember times when these memories would come to life. Dancing in visions so full of colour, before I had James.'

'Let me bring one of the memories to life now,' James said.

'Quite right, boy. We must show Eliza what her son will be able to do.'

James opened one of the dusty boxes. Inside of it he found numerous diaries. He opened one of the diaries at a random page.

'Ah this is from my grandfather,' James said.

'Ah, my father was such a great morph man,' Earl said.

James read from the diary, telling the tale of how on a cold December night, James's grandfather had told a girl named Betty that he loved her. As James read from the diary, images of the girl and her long red hair entered the basement, as though ghosts were acting out the story.

The girl named Betty was beautiful. James read how she was a witch and had looked down her nose at James's grandfather, whose magic didn't come from spells like hers. She had rejected his love.

'You're not good enough for me,' spoke the apparition from the journal. 'Leave me alone, or I'll put a hex on you.'

The diary entry ended with James's grandfather writing how he was heartbroken.

'Well, whoever she was, she certainly wasn't my mother,' said Earl with a chuckle. 'My mother Ericka was a good morph woman.'

Eliza was shaken to see the vision from James's grandfather's past. Yet this is what life would be like for her now. Visions and magic.

The family home in Locgarden was grand, yet James left the property, leaving Earl to sleep in his home there for the first time in over three decades.

James showed Eliza his home in Locgarden, which was a fair distance away from the house James had grown up in. They journeyed to James's house via a magic carpet.

Sitting on a magic carpet turned the riders invisible to the non-magical residents of Locgarden. It was a thrill to ride through the air, the feeling of the wind kissing her face.

Eliza spent the night with James in his home. She felt anxious being in this world, which was new and alien to her. She struggled to sleep.

'Come, my love, we will have more time to visit again soon. The baby requires that you rest.'

'I'm sorry, James. It's just so strange, knowing I'm in another dimension.'

'Let's go home and sleep in our beds in London. We can always visit my father again tomorrow if you're up to it.'

With that, they returned to London. Eliza found that she was exhausted after all the mental energy she had expelled that day. She slept deeply that night.

Chapter Twenty

James was soon to be a father. Eliza was due to give birth to baby Kaleb any day now. They had chosen that name because it sounded strong and like someone who would be courageous.

Today, Agnes was to meet with James. He was excited to see her, yet sad to know that she would soon no longer be magically bound to him as his guide.

When Agnes arrived at his flat, she looked different. She wasn't dressed in her usual posh clothing and snazzy shoes. She was wearing a pair of tracksuit bottoms and a Guns N' Roses black T-shirt.

'James,' she said.

James went to hug Agnes but she froze. He motioned for her to enter his flat. Agnes perched on the sofa; she looked tired.

'Everything OK?' James asked.

Agnes nodded. 'I won't be your guide soon.'

'I know. I can't believe I'm going to be a dad.'

Agnes sighed deeply. 'I know you'll make an interesting dad, to say the least.'

'Half-morph, half-vampire. My Kaleb is certainly going to be an interesting child.'

'And don't forget that he'll have his mortal side.' Agnes's voice was void of its usual peppiness.

'Agnes, what's wrong?' James asked.

'Mandy will be here soon. I said I'd give her my notes about you when you were little.'

'The way you're talking, it's like I won't see you again after you're no longer my guide. You're going to stick around to watch Kaleb grow up, aren't you?' James asked, knowing that Agnes had the option to remain connected to her memories for as long as she should wish.

Agnes waved a dismissive hand. 'I will be ridding myself of the memories of you as soon as Kaleb is born and I am no longer your guide. I know that you have killed hundreds of innocent humans in Locgarden. I am disgusted by you.'

James was shocked. He had never told Agnes his secret and he was not sure how she had found out. She must have heard from someone in the realm.

'Who told you?'

'It's not important!' cried Agnes, her voice illustrating her suppressed rage. 'I was meant to teach you to harness your powers and also how to be a good morph man.'

'But I'm also a vampire,' James said weakly.

'Yes, but there are plenty of vampires who do not kill.'

James felt angry at Agnes. He wanted her to accept him but he knew she could never love him as a mother now.

'I am sorry,' James replied weakly.

'Sorry,' Agnes spat the word back. 'This is just a weak word for a weak morph man who let the darkness override him. Being morph is something you've almost completely ignored.'

James wanted to roar in reply to her, to express how his vampire nature felt stronger than the experience of shapeshifting. Drinking blood was much more of a powerful sensation than stopping time or making an image appear out of thin air.

'As soon as the baby is born, I will move on from you. I will not stay around to watch you bring him up. I will move on and hope that my next charge isn't a dark soul like you are,' Agnes growled.

Agnes and James remained in silence while they waited for Mandy to arrive. There was so much James wanted to say to Agnes, yet he felt too broken to express himself.

What could he say? Agnes knew that he was a killer. This had been a secret he had kept from her for a lifetime. He had kept up an image of being a good man, yet they both knew that was a lie.

James was not just the shiny, confident person that the people of this world believed him to be. He was also a selfish killer who only cared about his loved ones and his own needs. Everyone else in this world and the magical realm was a commodity to be used.

When Mandy arrived, she was dressed in a green dress and black trendy coat. She was a slender woman who looked to be in her early twenties. She had dyed pink hair that was cut just above shoulder length. Her face was pretty and friendly.

'You must be James?' Mandy asked.

'Come on in,' James replied, sounding flat.

'Um, thanks,' Mandy said, as she followed him into the flat.

Agnes got up at once and threw her arms around Mandy. 'I'm so glad to see you,' Agnes said, huffing.

'Would you like something to drink?' James asked Mandy.

'I'm fine,' Mandy said. 'Agnes has filled me in about how the child will have vampire heritage as well. I don't remember my previous charges, of course … you know how it works. Anyway, I am going to give you my word that I will be dedicated to training Kaleb in his morph powers.'

'Of course,' James said with a sigh.

James felt sad as he thought about the morph aspect of his life. As soon as the baby was born, James would never be able to shapeshift or stop time. He already felt that these things were much more difficult because his morph powers were being drawn into the new baby.

He didn't want to change into a wolf again, knowing it could induce the pregnancy early as his powers were tied to the child. Yet in his mind he remembered clearly how he would run through the woods of Locgarden and feel so alive. He remembered the thrill of being his favourite animal to change into.

'Mandy, you are in the safe hands of James … Eliza will be here soon. I trust you are comfortable?' Agnes asked.

'Yes, thanks, I'll be fine,' said Mandy, beaming.

'I wish you all the best, I really do,' Agnes said. Agnes turned to look at James. 'Goodbye, James. I pray you change your ways, I really do.'

James didn't respond as he watched Agnes let herself out of the flat. He felt shaken to his core, imagining how he would never see his guide again.

'I want you to promise me something, Mandy, that you will not tell Eliza that this baby is part-vampire. For if you do, I will punish you. She does not need to know. I will train the child to contain its urges until a time should come when she grows old and dies of a mortal death.'

Mandy's lip trembled. 'OK, James, I promise. It's none of my business regarding the vampire aspect of this baby. My only concern with Kaleb is teaching him about his morph powers and our beliefs and teachings.'

'Then that's fine,' James said.

Mandy and James had little to say. They waited for Eliza to come home. It was clear that Eliza was shocked to see how youthful Mandy looked.

Mandy informed Eliza about some of the baby's powers and how she would help the child harness them from the elements around them.

'I am going to like having you around,' Eliza said, as Mandy prepared to leave.

'I'll see you again when Kaleb is born,' Mandy said, beaming as she bid James and Eliza farewell.

That night, Eliza and James watched television together. James had a glass of strong red wine and allowed himself to quietly brood the absence of Agnes in his life.

When Eliza asked him how Agnes was, he brushed off the question, stating how it was too much for him to deal with at present.

The evening was peaceful, yet James felt horrible inside. He wondered to himself whether he could become a changed man. Would he stop killing in Locgarden when Kaleb was born? He didn't know if he could. He was addicted to the blood and the images that would rush through his mind.

He wasn't sure whether his desire to please Agnes was strong enough now that he knew she would no longer be a part of his life. Even if she chose not to forget him and move onto a new charge, he still felt as though it would be a struggle for him to change his ways.

Chapter Twenty-one

Eliza's giving birth to baby Kaleb was smooth. In the quiet hospital in Locgarden, she was taken care of by the most professional and supernaturally inclined midwives and doctors.

Eliza was given a special drink brewed by the most enlightened of witches, which allowed her to feel no pain during childbirth. It was like a blurry dream giving birth to baby Kaleb. She felt the necklace upon her neck glow and exude heat for a moment as the child easily passed out of her and into the hands of the smiling midwife.

'What a beautiful … morph child,' said the midwife, smiling.

'Yes, he's half-mortal, too,' Eliza whispered.

'Half a lot of things, he is.' She took the baby and cleaned him up.

Eliza felt weak without the magic inside her body that had sustained her for nine months. She knew that the child had left enough magic in her that the necklace would belong to her always. She was a member of the magical realm for life.

Once the baby was cleaned up and put into a cot next to Eliza, James was permitted to enter the room. He kissed Eliza on the forehead and looked at his son with awe.

'My boy will grow up strong, wise and certainly handsome,' James said, beaming.

'I plan to teach him all about the art world. How to find his own voice through art,' Eliza whispered weakly.

'He will be a prodigious artist, no doubt,' James said, beaming. 'How are you feeling, my love?'

'I feel … exhausted. That witches' brew made me so blurry, if that word describes it adequately. I need to rest for just a little while. Look after Kaleb for me?'

'Of course, my sweet one. Mandy is here, too. She will see that this little morph comes to no harm, as will I,' James said, beginning to cry. 'You are very much aware that I am as mortal as you now. My morph legacy has been handed onto the next generation. I can feel the magic flowing out of me and entering Kaleb.'

'You will enjoy this realm the way I have over the last month. Like someone half-amazed and half-terrified by all the strange possibilities it possesses. Yet we will do it together … James, I must rest.'

James kissed Eliza once more on the forehead. Eliza noticed how Mandy had entered the room. Eliza believed that the young-looking Mandy would be a great guide. She wondered how old the girl really was.

As Mandy and James took care of the newborn baby now sleeping, taking the child into another room where it would be safe and overlooked by the finest doctors, Eliza herself fell into a deep slumber.

There she dreamt a dream that she knew was more than a simple dream. She saw the image of Kaleb; she knew his essence from the distinct feeling of his magic.

He was entering a class at the supernatural school he attended in Locgarden. Yet it wasn't a class for a morph child. It was a class for a child who held vampire descent.

The dream then took her into the past, where it showed young James and a blonde-haired girl at school. The blonde-haired girl passed young James a vial of blood and he drank it, revealing fangs.

Eliza knew what this meant and it saddened her greatly. He had been lying to her about his true heritage as a supernatural being. Yet the dream revealed no more about the future or the past.

Eliza slept for some time, yet she did not forget the revelation when she awoke. It was only when Earl came to pay his blessings on the birth of his grandson that she was able to confront the truth.

'The child looks just like James did when he was a baby.'

'He's mortal now, so to speak, James that is,' Eliza said, feeling dark sensations of anger.

'Quite,' Edgar said, looking down at the floor of the hospital.

'Surely it's not possible that I had a revelation, which revealed the amount of lies that this family tells … Is it true that James is part-vampire?'

Earl coughed and looked seriously at Eliza. 'He should have told you. It wasn't my place to reveal such things.'

'So, what of my child? Is Kaleb part-vampire?'

'The child will be a better man than James has ever been. He has mortal blood running alongside that of his morph and vampire lineage.'

Eliza was dumbstruck. Her child was also part-vampire. She knew little about the vampires that lived in this realm, yet they were one of the more frightening supernatural species.

'I will love this child. I will do everything to ensure that he becomes a good man. Tell me, Earl, what sort of man is James? Because you always say this child will be better than him.'

'These things are dangerous for even me to discuss. Leave them be; there's nothing you could do about them even if you knew.'

'Fine. Just promise me that you'll make sure Kaleb grows up to be a good person,' Eliza said.

'I promise that with every breath in my body,' Earl said.

*****

When Eliza returned to Earth a few days later, she felt like a new woman. She was the mother of a young baby who belonged to this world because of his grandparents and aunt Jessica. Yet he was also part-morph and part-vampire, and this would very much shape his life.

Eliza was glad to be back at the flat in Chelsea. She was glad to place baby Kaleb in the cot, which belonged to his safe place on Earth.

Kaleb had kind eyes and gazed upon her with the curiosity that a newborn baby has. Eliza believed that he would be a good child. She believed his vampire heritage would not make him evil. She was already educated on how noble and void of darkness half of the vampires in the magical realm were. Those were the vampires that Eliza would become acquainted with one day.

'My beautiful boy,' Eliza said with a sigh, as she looked upon her son.

Eliza got her iPhone out and took a snap of Kaleb. She sent it to Jessica's and her parents' mobiles. She knew they would have been eagerly awaiting news on the new baby.

Moreen called her back shortly after. Eliza's mother was always on her phone and had a lot of friends.

'My dear girl,' Moreen said on the phone.

'Hi, Mum, it's so good to hear from you.'

'Oh, the boy's got James's good looks. I'm a proud grandmother.'

'Thanks, Mum.'

'Tell me, was your labour painful? Are you OK, my dear?'

'I had a really smooth labour. Kaleb's three days old. We've got a nanny to help with the childcare, her name's Mandy.' It was much simpler to describe Kaleb's magical guide as a nanny.

'Oh, wonderful. Have you checked that she's a good egg?'

'Yes, Mum. She was recommended from one of James's friends and is covered by a good agency,' Eliza embellished the reality. Magical guides came from a mystical place in the heavens on the magical realm, and were connected to the elements just like the power of morphs were.

'I love you so much, dear. I will visit soon. I can't wait to see him,' Moreen said, her voice bright.

'Yes, Mum. How about you visit next week?'

'Of course. I'll text you to arrange a day. Love you loads. Talk soon, love,' Moreen said.

After the call, Eliza was on her own again with her magical child. Mandy was in the spare room and there if Eliza needed any company. Yet she wanted to be a normal mum in these moments.

Chapter Twenty-two

Ten years passed. The year was now 2029. Eliza was in her late thirties and Kaleb was soon to be ten years old. In just a matter of days, he would have his tenth birthday.

Through the magical powers that Mandy possessed, she appeared to grow older to the world. All of Eliza's family regarded her well.

Eliza knew that her child was half-vampire, yet she kept it secret from James that she knew. Over the years, the revelation that she had experienced at Kaleb's birth – that James was in fact the biggest liar she had ever met – had changed the way she saw her now husband.

They had married shortly after Kaleb's birth. Eliza remembered how dearly she had once loved James. Yet even on their wedding day, she had experienced feelings of doubt. She was afraid of what truths James may be keeping hidden from her. She was sure that he was one of the good vampires. She believed he was ashamed of his vampire heritage because morphs were known for hating vampires.

Kaleb was a lovely child. He was always smiling and friendly. He had a light about him that made Eliza sure he would always be as pure as he was at present.

Mandy was teaching him basic magic for now, unlike Agnes, who had taught James complex tricks such as stopping time when he was only a young boy.

Mandy would teach Kaleb how to make a butterfly appear in his room. The little boy would clap and laugh as the creature fluttered around.

Eliza worked in an art gallery in London. It was an independent studio that was not particularly popular. Most of the art was from students and people who, although talented, were in no way famous. Eliza loved her work. It made her feel connected to her path in life before magic.

She would paint regularly and with passion. She enjoyed trying to explore different styles with the work she created in each realm.

Eliza was a proud aunt to Jessica's children. Jessica was still happily married to Bradley and had two daughters. Hattie was seven and Minnie was aged four. They lived in their smart house in Chesham. Bradley no longer worked and was learning to speak Japanese.

Life was good. Eliza spent a third of her time in the magical realm. Even Kaleb was nervous the first time he was old enough to understand that he was entering a different reality.

The magical realm was full of flying carpets. Witches and warlocks. It was a vast world that was so different from Earth.

*****

James was excited to think that his son would be ten soon. He was in awe at how kind and decent Kaleb was.

He remembered himself as a child. He often wondered if he would have been a different man had he not met Maggie.

He often secretly talked with Kaleb. He didn't tell him what sort of vampire he really was, yet he explained how there were bad vampires. He expressed how Kaleb must not become one of these vampires because they were foul creatures.

James was excited to prepare for Kaleb's birthday parties. He had already got Kaleb a large teddy bear and a toy car set for his party on Earth. He had wrapped them up and put them in the cupboard. He and Eliza still lived in the same flat in Chelsea that James had owned since turning eighteen.

As James walked through the witches' market in Locgarden, he wondered to himself what to get his son for the party in Locgarden. Earl would be there, along with some of the teachers and students from Kaleb's school for supernatural children.

James didn't know that Eliza knew his secret identity as a vampire. He often told Kaleb not to play with vampire children. Yet between James and Kaleb, the two discussed what it meant to be a vampire.

Kaleb's bloodlust hadn't yet formed, which could possibly indicate he had a low bloodlust for a vampire. This would be a blessing in keeping the child a moral being.

The witches' market was full of weird and wonderful stools. All the witches looked different. To passers-by, they looked like they were selling antiques or craft items, yet their hidden products were spells, magical items and services for the supernatural beings of Locgarden.

James still visited the evil witch Brandy so that he could enter the Kitchen. Yet today, he was shopping for his son and steered well away from her stall.

He knew that a witch called Mischa sold magical items that were considered blessed. She was one of the kind and good witches of the city.

When James arrived at Mischa's stall, the beautiful witch's face fell into a frown.

'I'm looking for a present for my son,' James said.

'Errr … are you sure you want my services?' Mischa asked.

'Yes, I'm sure,' barked James.

Mischa bit her lip. 'Can I see a picture of your son?'

James got out his phone for this realm. Technology in the realm matched Earth's, as magical beings had taken the advancements of phones and other gadgets to the realm.

'Hmmm, your son is a being of light,' Mischa said.

'I know. I want a present that is blessed,' James replied.

The witch presented a child's watch. The watch was a silver object with red charms. It looked modern yet expensive.

'What does it do?' James asked.

'Apart from telling the time, the watch will help your son stay blessed throughout time. It will also grow as he ages. He will be able to wear it on his wrist now as a little boy, and when he becomes a man it will fit him as well.'

James handed the witch money for the watch. Her hands were shaking as she took the money and handed it to him.

He walked off pleased that he had a perfect gift for Kaleb's party. The party was to be tomorrow night in the realm. Eliza and Kaleb were already at the house preparing for it.

James felt happy as he walked back to his house. By the time he got home, he was hot and wished to have a long shower.

When he arrived, Eliza was watching the news. Kaleb was sitting on the purple fabric sofa and conjuring butterflies to dance around him. The little boy was clapping and giggling.

As soon as he saw his father, Kaleb jumped off the sofa and the butterflies disappeared.

'Daddy, you're home,' Kaleb said.

James hugged his son, asking, 'Are you excited for your party?'

'Yes, Daddy. I invited my friends and they are going to watch me make butterflies dance in the air.'

James smiled, commenting, 'Good boy.'

Eliza turned off the television and got up to kiss James on the lips. 'Mandy's going to conjure up the most amazing tea,' Eliza said, laughing softly.

'Are you not going to go and buy the food then?' asked James with a laugh.

'No, we certainly are not. We will show off like a proud young morph should,' Eliza said with a giggle.

'Well, that sounds fair enough. Let's go and get Mandy; she can conjure up some fairies to dance in the decorations as well.'

Kaleb ran into the spare room where Mandy stayed. He came back holding the young woman's hand. His little eyes were full of excitement.

James greeted Mandy and told her to help Kaleb to conjure the butterflies. The little boy wasn't yet able to make fairies appear or do other such tricks. He was a little bit of a slow learner with his magical abilities.

The doorbell rang and James knew it was his father. He walked to the door to greet Earl. The old man smiled with a tired expression as he entered the house.

'How's my little grandson doing?' he asked Kaleb.

'Fine, Granddaddy. We are going to have presents first, Dad says, so the other children don't get jealous.'

'Very good,' Earl said, as he produced a small wooden car painted in faint colours.

'Is it magical?' asked Kaleb, beaming.

'It's a good luck charm, my boy; it maintains a person's good merit. Perhaps I should have given one of these to your daddy, as he's an awful man,' said Earl with a laugh. 'Of course, I'm only being silly.' Yet Earl looked seriously at James for a second as he said this.

'Daddy, what did you get me?' asked little Kaleb.

James fetched the watch. He explained to Kaleb how it was blessed and would adapt to his style and change with his age.

'A watch that will last forever!' shouted Kaleb with excitement in his voice.

'Forever is a long time,' Eliza commented, laughing.

'Forever and ever and ever!' shouted Kaleb with joy.

The party was enjoyable. Mandy conjured the fairies to dance and sing. They were not real fairies, as those were found in swamp land and wouldn't be so cooperative. Yet the magic looked so real. All the children were impressed.

Kaleb had one other child come to his party. The rest of his class had declined the invitation. James wondered if Kaleb was maybe unpopular at school. He recalled how at his school on Earth, none of the children had come, yet Kaleb had seemed so contented to play with his cousins.

The little child that came to the party was a werewolf. He had long brown hair. The child talked a great deal about how he could turn into a wolf when it was a full moon. James thought the child was very annoying, yet he was glad that Kaleb had a friend at school.

Chapter Twenty-three

James didn't often meet up with Maggie. Over the years, they would meet up roughly once every year. She had her own life working in the research on ancient vampire history. She was immersed in her research.

It was fascinating to hear about when James did meet up with Maggie. Her eyes would light up with excitement as she recounted how the archaeology teams had found all sorts of ancient relics in the city.

James was feeling good. Things were going well. Eliza was none the wiser to the fact that he was a vampire. Or at least that is what he believed.

He was glad that he was alone in the house in Locgarden today. Eliza and Kaleb were on Earth. He would catch up with them in what would feel like a couple of days to him.

When Maggie arrived, he was pleased to meet her. She was dressed in a long hippy-style dress, which was the fashion at present all over the realm. She looked elegant.

'Oh, good to see you, old buddy,' Maggie said, as she hugged him.

'It always feels like such a long time since we last reunited,' James replied.

'We are always missing each other in the Kitchen. I ask the new staff about you all the time. They will exclaim how I've just missed you the other day, always the same,' said Maggie with a laugh.

As Maggie and James prepared to enter the Kitchen, they discussed what was going on in each of their lives. Maggie expressed how she had a new man in her life. He was a vampire whom was Maggie's elder by 200 years. She expressed how impressed she was with his interest for their kind's history and how attractive he was.

Things had changed since the days when James and Maggie were required to visit Brandy to enter the Kitchen. Now all they needed to do was book it in advance by texting her. She was expecting them to enter and had given them a charm that allowed them to enter in their own homes. It worked on a similar type of magic to their invisible keys.

Throwing the small charm on the floor allowed the item to temporarily break. The charm was shaped like a small marble elephant. The item broke and the portal that allowed them to enter the Kitchen was opened. James's house blurred away as the two vampires entered the Kitchen.

James had the repaired elephant ornament in his hands. It was their way to get out of the Kitchen when they desired to leave.

The Kitchen always looked the same – purple décor and modern booths for vampires to feed. All the feeding was discrete and no one could view the goings on from outside the booth.

There were curvy vampire dancers in corsets in cages. The women looked beautiful and sensual as they swayed to the music that was playing. It was sensual music.

'We're finally back here together,' Maggie said, beaming.

'It feels good to be doing this with you; I guess I'll never get tired of what our friendship equates to,' said James with a laugh.

'Me neither. Just like the old days in school.'

A pretty ginger waitress came up to the two of them. She was wearing a PVC black corset dress. James could tell that she had recently fed and was feeling the buzz of working there. She was younger than they were. The Kitchen tended to employ young, pretty vampires to be their waitresses.

'Hi,' said the ginger vampire. 'I've seen you before,' she said, addressing James. 'Would you two like a double booth or a single one each?'

'Single, please,' James said.

As the waitress turned on her heels to book the booth, there was a loud crash.

'Oh, what was that?' asked the waitress.

Heavy footsteps could be heard walking slowly. No one was alarmed until a magical stake pierced the waitress's heart and she turned to dust.

Maggie screamed and clung to James for protection. 'Get us out of here,' she hissed.

As James produced the elephant ornament from his jacket pocket, he heard the laughter again as a dizzying sensation hit him.

'Pretty creatures. Bloody sport in here,' said the vampire hunter.

James's heart was pounding as he realised the imminent danger that he was in. Yet the vampire hunter had put her powers over him. He was no longer morph, so he could not easily wash them away.

'Look at the pretty vampires, standing helplessly afraid,' said the hunter, as she walked out of her hiding place. She was a beautiful black woman with long hair. Her hair was worn in black and purple braids. She had her nose pierced and was dressed in combat trousers and a black top.

'Please,' begged Maggie.

The vampire hunter laughed. 'Can't move, can you? Afraid I might hurt you. Little frightened vampire, are we?'

James was petrified. This was how his mother Stephanie must have felt.

The vampire hunter revealed another stake and hurled it into Maggie's heart. She screamed as she turned to dust.

Years of memories rushed through James's mind as he felt his life flashing before his eyes. He thought of meeting Maggie in school and how they had always loved this place. Maggie had carved him into the man that he was today. Now she was dust on the floor.

Something inside him turned in the seconds that passed. Something that didn't belong to him. Something he knew was borrowed from Kaleb, because it was morph power. It was just enough power to cut the magic that the hunter had over him and break the elephant.

As the seconds passed that the huntress was about to speak, stating how she would kill him, the room faded away and he found himself back in his house. He was shaking and sweating.

Maggie was dead! Maggie had been killed by a vampire hunter. He could never enter the Kitchen again.

He knew he was no longer safe in this place. What if the vampire hunter caught up with him and was able to trace his magic back to his home?

James nervously switched on his computer in his home in Locgarden. He had to get out of this city. Here he would be in danger in the realm. For as long as a vampire hunter was chasing him, he would be royally fucked.

He thought of cities where he could run to. Countries he could elope to. Yet it sounded too much. They spoke different languages in those places and he knew that it would be too much for Eliza and Kaleb.

'I'm fucked, fucked, fucked,' James said, as he typed in faraway towns on a property-buying site.

He knew that the hunter wouldn't expect him to be in a poor town. Somewhere less extravagant than Locgarden. Yet it was also somewhere where

Stephanie's sister lived. Maybe she could help James.

He had no time to call her. He simply had to do what he thought was best. This is why James bought the first reasonable house he found on the property site. He felt his key become hot as its magic was transferred to take him to the town of Mempesh whenever he entered the realm.

His new house was a small two-bedroom property on an old-fashioned street. It was on the other side of Mempesh to where Stephanie's sister Lexi lived. He would call upon her and ask her to help. He knew she was the same kind of vampire as he was. He felt she was the only person who could help him.

'I'll call upon Aunt Lexi,' James said. The deed was done. His house in Locgarden was no longer connected to the magical key. Although it was still his home, he no longer had it ascertained as his first place of residence in the realm.

'Mempesh,' James mused, trying to calm himself. He opened the doorway back to Earth, knowing he must leave the scene now. He couldn't risk the vampire hunter catching him. He knew she could follow him no further than the realm. He had sensed her magic wasn't as powerful as the hunter who had killed his mother. He was glad it wasn't the same person. He remembered that hunter's magic because he had felt it eleven years ago when his father had shown him the memory.

*****

A day passed on Earth where James didn't mention that their magical keys would now take them to Mempesh. He was anxious to break the news to Eliza.

He feared how she would complain that Kaleb was struggling to make friends. He would find it hard to start a new school.

Yet as he lay in bed next to her, he saw her touch her magical key. He grabbed her hand and felt the softness of her skin.

'I have something to tell you,' he said, knowing he'd have to tell her sooner or later.

'What is it?' Eliza asked with a smile.

'I've bought us a house in Mempesh. You'll love it. I've moved our geographical place in the realm. When you enter, you'll see what a charming property it is. It's away from all the hustle of the city.'

'Shouldn't you have mentioned this to me? You didn't sell your home there did you? Well?'

'No … I …'

'Then we can just move to Mempesh when Kaleb goes to high school. He needs his friend

Milton. You know that boy's his only friend at either of his schools.'

James sighed deeply, saying, 'Woman, just trust me.'

Eliza laughed almost hysterically. 'Trust you? You mean to say that I should just trust that you've suddenly moved after all this time?'

'What's that supposed to mean?'

Eliza hopped out of bed and produced a journal. In it she had written down how she had known about James's vampire heritage since Kaleb was first born. Nervous energy ran through James's mind as he thought of how she had known for a decade.

'Why didn't you say sooner?' was all that James could muster to say.

'I don't know. I suppose I thought I should stay with you until Kaleb was older,' Eliza said, as she burst into tears.

This was a revelation that James had not expected. He had never in his whole relationship with Eliza expected it to fall apart. First Maggie had died on him, and now the love of his life was expressing how she one day wanted to leave him.

James at once felt a maddening anger come over him. He at once drew out his key and dragged the two of them into the house in Mempesh.

Eliza screamed. James watched her nervously look around the house. He didn't know what he was thinking. He couldn't let her leave him. Thoughts of how she might take Kaleb away spun through his mind.

'You can't leave me!' he shouted.

'I've always said to myself that I'll stay until Kaleb is eighteen. I'll make sure he is a good man, unlike the monster I married.'

James felt hot anger and hatred for the hungry being he had become all those years ago. A being that had been created by his vampiric lust. He knew Maggie had only been the catalyst and perhaps he would have always gone down this dark and bloodthirsty road.

He felt fear that everything was crumbling around him as he drank in Eliza's aura. She had hidden secrets from him. He could feel how she no longer loved him in the same way. She had used a weak charm to hide this fact, yet now that magic was broken with the revelation of the truth.

James felt mad with excitement. He believed he could change Eliza's mind by turning her. She would be the second women he had turned. Yet he knew it was from a place of needing her, wanting to keep dear Eliza forever, that he would take such an action.

As he delved into her, he felt the great bloodlust, yet he was able to control it and not kill her. He drank slowly as she screamed into his clothing. She weakly fell and was unable to stop herself from drinking the blood that he forced into her mouth.

As she lay in an unmade bed in the newly bought house in Mempesh, she convulsed and shook. The bed was second-hand and stank. The house was cheap and unclean.

James had felt it was the perfect place to escape the vampire hunter. It was his only chance of keeping his family safe. He knew that the hunter would not be after Kaleb, yet he was a killer and all hunters despised the sort of vampire that he was.

Eliza slept soundly for a day and a night. James simply watched her. He occasionally drank black coffee. He felt sure that she would love him the way she used to when she woke.

Yet when she awoke, she was cold. 'Take me home to my son,' she said.

'Do you wish to feed?' James asked.

'I shall do no such thing. I shall never take life. This is a curse for me, and yet to know I will live forever with Kaleb as my son is also a blessing. I believe I am glad that you have done this, yet I must return to him. I cannot be in this place with you.'

James explained to her that she would need to rest. He said he would have to assess if she had a strong bloodlust before she entered Earth again.

They spent days together. In that time, they painted the house a clean white colour, as the walls had been painted a dirty green and purple.

James told Eliza all about the Kitchen in Locgarden and how his school friend Maggie had been killed by a vampire hunter. He told her about the evil witch Brandy, who had given him access to the Kitchen. Eliza said she would stay with James until Kaleb was eighteen, yet there was a strange look in her eyes that James could no longer read.

*****

When Eliza returned to Earth as a vampire with James, days passed until she filed for divorce. James was a broken man, yet he knew it was his fault for the person he had become.

Kaleb cried and cried at the news. Not only that, but Eliza took Kaleb away to live in Swansea, where she bought a two-bedroom property and applied to become an art teacher.

As James watched Eliza pack, he sat in silence. Mandy tended to Kaleb, who had to be quelled with a magical influence. The child was in great hurt at the fact his parents were divorcing. He had made it begin to rain in the flat that James would now live alone in once again.

James felt numb. He didn't know who he would become now. Eliza had promised that he could see his son whenever he liked. His son would live with him in Mempesh in the magical realm. Yet on Earth, Kaleb would start at another new school in Swansea.

*****

Eliza had always loved Swansea. Before she ever met James, she often looked at properties online in the city. It had been one of the places she had aspired to one day move to. Yet it had only ever been a dream. Yet now, she had the push to move. Things were over with James. She was a single woman and a vampire. Mandy had promised her that they would find a good witch that would help her appear as though she was aging to her friends and family on Earth.

This way, she could watch them grow old and live their lives. When she thought of watching Jessica die and knowing that she would never see her again after that, her heart hurt.

Their spirits no longer belonged to the same celestial realm. So, when her family died, that would be it; they would not be reunited in the beyond, which the witches promised existed.

Eliza had paid £70,000 for a two-bedroom terrace in Swansea. It was in a good yet working-class area. It was the sort of place she felt was such a contrast from the millionaire property that James lived in, yet it felt more beautiful to her than James's flat ever could.

The house felt warm and loving. Mandy moved out and rented a flat nearby. She was working part-time in Costa when she was not teaching Kaleb how to become the best morph that he could be.

As the weeks went by, it was awkward when she visited James to drop off Kaleb in Mempesh in the realm. Eliza liked the town, which was slower than the crazy city of Locgarden.

Kaleb was struggling in both his new schools. He was healing, with the help of Mandy, and learning to accept that his parents no longer loved each other in the same way.

*****

One year later.

Kaleb was doing better in school. At his school in Swansea, he had a few friends. He was eleven now and starting high school; where he lived, it started in year seven.

He didn't go to a private school in either Mempesh (as the town was too poor to have one) or Swansea. The young boy was having a very different upbringing to James.

Kaleb was an innocent child. He was very sweet-natured and this was something that James cherished in him.

James had not killed anyone since Maggie had died. He was planning on having a witch curse him soon, so that he could never kill another person. He had told Eliza about this and she had asked that the same witch curse her, as well, even though she had not killed anyone as a vampire.

'We should curse Kaleb, too,' Eliza said.

'You are right, I will get Fifi to do this.'

'We are all immortal. This curse is our gift. To live an immortal life void of any more sin. It is the most beautiful gift an immortal can receive.'

James would arrange for Fifi to come at once to the house in Mempesh. Eliza was staying the night and it almost felt like old times. She even smiled at him, which was rare, as she usually no longer made any more eye contact with him.

When the short witch with long brown hair and dark eyes came to the house, she bowed and smiled. 'You won't regret this. This is a gift that I bring.'

James knew that Fifi was right. James would never again be able to feed on a human. He would live forever, yet never take another life.

He knew that Fifi had told him he could still turn someone. It was a clause that they had discussed privately. James knew he wanted love again and believed he would find it in immortality. Yet Fifi had made it so that anyone he turned would also not be able to kill.

A smile grew on James's face as he welcomed Fifi in to perform the life-changing spell.

The End